He couldn't hold off the enemy

Katz squeezed off another shot, then ducked as a fresh barrage sent stinging chips of concrete flying against his cheek. He was cornered and had no hope of returning fire measure for measure. Clearly he couldn't stop the enemy's relentless advance.

Abruptly they stopped the forward press, and Katz cautiously peered out. He spotted a car moving slowly down the street, and at even intervals behind it, five more. The vehicles reminded him of a strange funeral procession—headlights off but with small winglike flares waving from the top of the side windows.

Several Russians broke ranks to check out the first car, and they trotted alongside, trying to use it for cover. Katz tracked the gun on one, ready to pull the trigger. But he was spared the trouble. The darkness was dissolved by an explosion.

Mack Bolan's

PHOENIX FORCE.

#1 Argentine Deadline
#2 Guerilla Games
#3 Atlantic Scramble
#4 Tigers of Justice
#5 The Fury Bombs
#6 White Hell
#7 Dragon's Kill
#8 Aswan Hellbox
#9 Ultimate Terror
#10 Korean Killground
#11 Return to Armageddon
#12 The Black Alchemists
#13 Harvest Hell
#14 Phoenix in Flames
#15 The Viper Factor
#16 No Rules, No Referee
#17 Welcome to the Feast
#18 Night of the Thuggee
#19 Sea of Savages
#20 Tooth and Claw
#21 The Twisted Cross
#22 Time Bomb
#23 Chip Off the Bloc
#24 The Doomsday Syndrome
#25 Down Under Thunder
#26 Hostaged Vatican
#27 Weep, Moscow, Weep
#28 Slow Death
#29 The Nightmare Merchants
#30 The Bonn Blitz
#31 Terror in the Dark
#32 Fair Game
#33 Ninja Blood
#34 Power Gambit
#35 Kingston Carnage
#36 Belgrade Deception
#37 Show of Force

PHOENIX FORCE®

GAR WILSON

SHOW OF FORCE

A GOLD EAGLE BOOK FROM
WORLDWIDE®

TORONTO • NEW YORK • LONDON • PARIS
AMSTERDAM • STOCKHOLM • HAMBURG
ATHENS • MILAN • TOKYO • SYDNEY

First edition September 1988

ISBN 0-373-61337-7

Special thanks and acknowledgment to
Dan Streib for his contribution to this work.

Printed in U.S.A.

1

"Just what the hell is Cheyenne, Wyoming, doing inside the USSR?" Yakov Katzenelenbogen exclaimed in whispered Russian.

Neither of the two men with him spoke any Slavic language fluently, but they shared his surprise. It was eerie. They looked at the town the way they would at a coral snake with its beautiful geometric rings.

"Bloody hell," the man to Katzenelenbogen's left said softly. "There's even a church."

His name was David McCarter. A graduate of England's prestigious Sandhurst Military Academy and a dropout from Britain's highly decorated Glosters Army Division, he thrived on danger. He craved action the way others craved food, and he had "found himself" in Phoenix Force, America's ultrasecret five-man strike team. America's Foreign Legion, McCarter called it sometimes. The President often sent the order that put the team into action, but it was never openly linked to him or anyone else officially in the government.

In the field the team was led by Yakov Katzenelenbogen, or Katz as his friends called him rather than attempt a tongue-tying pronunciation of his last name.

And McCarter was right, Katz thought. They were in the heart of Russia, which, according to Party dogma, was manifestly atheist, and in the distance before them sparkled a quaint white church with a tall steeple that seemed to reach for the slowly darkening sky. The scene could have been plucked directly from a Norman Rockwell painting.

Anywhere else the structure would stand as a symbol of peace and friendly neighbors, but there in the south of Communist Russia, it seemed to be an ominous mockery that could turn into a trap for Phoenix Force.

"Curious," the third man said. "Quite an anachronism, a new church inside Russia. Are we to believe a revival of faith is encouraged here?"

The third and last man in the Phoenix Force detachment was a Canadian, Gary Manning, a thirty-four-year-old plastic explosives expert.

Two more Phoenix Force shock troopers remained behind as a reserve. They were twenty miles away at a luxurious tourist hotel designed to attract the hard currencies carried by visitors from the capitalist West.

The two were not real tourists, of course. If Katz and his detachment did not return on schedule, the reserves would rush north to help.

At the moment the three in the woods read a Chamber of Commerce sign on the only road leading into town: Welcome To Cheyenne, Wyoming, Where The New West Meets The Old.

Though the trio found their curiosity piqued by the macabre scene before them, they restrained themselves. They were not the kind of men who shy away from the unknown, and they wanted to crawl closer, but common sense and experience prevailed.

Armed guards might be hiding in the forest that surrounded the strange little clone. Trip mines or deadly electric lines might interlace in the deep underbrush near where they lay.

They had no idea what the existence of the strange town meant.

"I don't like it," Katz said.

A fifty-five-year-old Jew of Russian descent, he was skeptical of almost everything inside the Iron Curtain. And he was certain that the reason for the presence of prim and neatly painted homes and the two blocks of stores and shops was anything but benign.

Generally he took nothing for granted and observed more precautions than the other two, which was one reason he led the Phoenix Force team in the field.

"Well," David McCarter said as he started to rise, "let's go on a gander and have a look at this bit of western prosperity in Russia's economic moors."

Katz detained him with a touch to his arm.

Manning shared his companion's eagerness. Neither of them was timid. They were steeped in action, and by temperament they preferred to push on. It was hard to lie on their bellies, but they would be stretching orders if they moved another yard farther.

So they waited restlessly for Katz to train his field glasses on the scene below them. The small town that was an American look-alike was nestling under the shade of trees that spread out like a green umbrella over the buildings and the short, macadam-paved streets. He estimated that there were about a hundred houses with typical American small-town architecture, but not one of the drab walk-up apartment buildings that housed most of the Soviet citizens.

Retail establishments stretched for two blocks that could have passed for Main Street, U.S.A.

Several factory-type structures crowded the far edge of town. From one of the large buildings, the American team could hear a sharp pounding that sounded like rapid-action gunfire. Katz suspected it was an indoor firing range.

Beyond that was still another curiosity. An airport? Katz wondered.

But it wasn't exactly an airport. A hangar with open doors was empty. Three aircraft were parked near the end of the dirt runway.

The planes confounded him as much as the town. From the distance the aircraft looked as though they had been built by the Wright brothers.

"Komitet Gosudarstvennoi Bezopasnosti," said Gary Manning. "It's got to be some kind of KGB insane asylum."

"Maybe it's an elaborate dacha for the Communist Party bigwigs," McCarter suggested. "They probably like to sample the good life now and again."

Katz volunteered a reminder. "Figuring out what it's used for is outside our objectives. Headquarters wants one thing from us: a description that the spy satellites can't provide. And they want us out before we get snarled in a black widow's net of the KGB."

"To hell with objectives. Do we go closer or don't we?" the man with the English accent asked impatiently.

Baffled by what he saw, Katz perspired in spite of the cooling air that preceded the oncoming darkness.

He worried about the mission.

They had seen what they had come to decipher, and they ought to retreat while they were reasonably sure of escaping.

Already they had bloodied a mission that was supposed to be like a tourist trip.

Getting into Yalta had been easy. They traveled with a group of ordinary American families, and on the second day the three had slipped away from their eagle-eyed Intourist guide with relative ease.

Finding a car had proved more difficult. They had attempted to bribe a driver into relinquishing his state-owned vehicle without a struggle. In the end they had convinced the Russian by knocking him unconscious, perhaps killing him, and rolling him down an embankment.

Katz killed easily, but he killed only men who deserved to die or those who had to be sacrificed for the greater good.

Their mission, with a goal that seemed trivial compared to their usual tasks, would not justify killing except in self-defense.

But there was the faint sound of a breaking twig, and Katz knew the mission was due to take a sudden nasty twist.

He tapped his teammates on the shoulder. No words were necessary.

Gary Manning, the Canadian who lived in the bush whenever he could, pressed his ear to the ground. After a short while, he held up five fingers.

David McCarter cursed to himself. It seemed as though their cover would be blown, and it couldn't happen at a worse spot. Deep in the heart of Russia.

Katz, rotating his head from left to right, felt the same.

Immediately his teammates began to ease away from him.

It was time to break and run.

Katz, though, hated retreats, but an encounter with Russian guards could easily result in their information dying with them.

As he mulled over the decision, he could hear the rustling of clothing against the pine trees, and knew it was too late. They would be heard or seen regardless of how good they were at evasive tactics.

So he made the decision.

"Start walking," he whispered. "Toward the voices."

"Toward them?" McCarter questioned.

Gary Manning understood. He had walked toward black bears more than once and had threatened them with nothing more than a throaty grumble. When an animal refused to back away or started to charge, he killed the beast with the .44 Magnum he carried when he went fishing. The gun was meant for protection against vengeful human enemies that he had made during his stint in Phoenix Force, but it served equally well with bears and packs of wolves.

He wished he had the .44 now as the five men with rifles moved close enough to be clearly visible.

They wore some type of uniform, but not the military dress that Katz and the others had expected.

Chalk up another question mark, Katz thought. It was the damnedest mission he had ever been sent on.

The guns carried by the approaching Russians added to the questions. They did not carry their rifles by the slings or hold them at port arms. Instead they carried them in game hunter style with the stock under their armpit and muzzle pointed harmlessly at the ground.

But the Phoenix Force detachment continued inching apart, getting as much brush or trees between them as they could.

The Russians froze as they finally spotted the strangers in the woods. Immediately they turned. The three in the center rather automatically selected their own targets, while the two on either side scanned for other intruders.

That action alone indicated that they were not amateurs.

The situation was awkward to say the least, Katz thought. With no concealed weapons, not even the .22-caliber gun he usually wore in his artificial arm, he doubted he could jump even one of the armed men before he would draw a round of shots.

He looked for a strategy, checking the Russians' weapons immediately.

The shortest of the five men carried an Anschutz. A custom model, it was similar to the classic design except for the roll-over Monte Carlo cheek piece and the Wunderhammer palm swell on the pistol grip. It was a .22 or .222, hardly a weapon appropriate for guard duty. Two others carried Mossbergs and two carried Redfields, which looked to be special hand-engraved limited-edition showpiece models.

Very odd, Katz speculated. Innocent sportsmen.

Then he glanced at Gary Manning. His face was bright with anticipation.

The Canadian was a strange man. He had dedicated his life to fighting barbarians and crazed terrorists who constantly waged their deadly raids against the innocent and weak of the world. His dedication ranked with that of priests.

That's why he was on the Phoenix Force team.

But what had instilled that dedication in him was never clear.

Katz was concerned somewhat that the situation would get out of hand before they adequately determined the type of Russian men they confronted.

"Halt. Stop where you are." The man who snapped the order spoke in unaccented English.

That diverted Katz for only a second.

He broke into a broad smile, extended his good hand graciously and took several steps forward, effectively closing the distance between himself and the Russians.

He responded in a friendly manner with a Russian greeting.

The leader gave him a chastising look reminiscent of a stern father threatening a child. "Speak American, you fool. Haven't you been told often enough?"

"Well, yes," Katz replied, but he couldn't figure out what was going on. What was wrong with speaking Russian?

The eyes of the hunter narrowed to slits as he looked at Katz again. "Who are you anyway?" he demanded. "Newcomers?"

Katz answered, "*Da.* I mean, yes. Just got in today."

He took another step forward, feeling that he could take out the apparent leader, which left two apiece for Manning and McCarter.

They were on the move, too, but he could not see what steps they were taking to defend themselves. It was important that they avoided any shooting. Shots heard below in the village could bring an army of inhabitants into the game.

"I'm Jerry Swanson," Manning said. He extended a friendly hand to the man nearest him.

"Fred Hansen." McCarter smiled engagingly. He did not offer to shake hands, but Katz could see what he was doing. He had brushed a sapling aside and was using his body to hold it back like a slingshot.

Katz took a deep breath.

The Russian in front of him scowled.

"No one came in today. The bus is not due for a week."

"Well, you see..."

The Russian's expression blended a bit of surprise and a heavy dose of anger. "You lie...you..." The man raised his rifle an inch. It was as far as any of them got before the Phoenix Force team went into action.

McCarter ducked and let the sapling whip forward. Leaves and small branches slashed across the faces of the two men nearest him. They dodged and raised a hand to protect their eyes.

McCarter leaped right behind the branch. With his head down, he rammed his skull into one Russian's belly. Already off balance from the branches, the man staggered backward. The Briton easily wrenched the rifle from the falling man's hands. His other adversary, still adjusting to the surprise attack, was an easy target. McCarter swung the confiscated rifle like a cricket bat, shattering the man's right knee and swinging back for a crack at his face.

McCarter jackhammered the rifle butt into alternate skulls. Dazed looks and collapsing bodies announced the effectiveness of his technique.

Manning took a different tack. He held up his hands as if in surrender, but before the rifles could be raised to cover him, he snapped two dead limbs from the tree above him. He sprang at the men, taking a hockey goaltender's stance and driving between the Russians.

"Suppertime, gentlemen," he yelled.

He caught each of them at the waist, toppling them as they tried to raise their rifles. When they fell, Manning was on top of them. He thrust a six- to ten-inch stub into each man's open mouth.

They lost all capability to fight back. With both hands, each man fought to do one thing, to clear his air passage, but Manning, with a final thrust, finished them off.

An expert rifleman, self-taught in Canada's vast wilderness, he preferred to kill at a great distance, but the Russians had left him no choice. The act had been a bit bizarre, and reminded him of peasants dispatching vampires.

Manning looked away for a second, then his eyes found McCarter, who finished his work.

So had Katz. The "old man" of the group had finished his single opponent with relative ease. He had slashed a cross-body karate chop with one hand to knock the rifle barrel out of position. At the same time his prosthetic arm speared at the man's face. It jabbed the Russian's eye, driving it back into soft brain tissue.

In his agony the Russian tried to pull the hook from his face, ignoring the other hand that was clamped like a vise on his throat. He was still fighting to get the thing from his eye when he breathed his last.

When it was over, the three survivors surveyed their body count.

They did not celebrate.

In other missions, the justification was clear, but this assignment had seemed so trivial.

Thinking back, Katz remembered that it had started without the usual sense of danger. Now they were in the midst of serious trouble.

2

As he stood in the center of the minimassacre on the fringe of the phony Cheyenne, Wyoming, Katzenelenbogen remembered how different the mission had sounded in the beginning...

In fact, the assignment had sounded like a vacation. Katz had been summoned to a mission briefing at Stony Man Farm. The message was cryptic and had intrigued him.

> You are cordially invited to spend this coming weekend at Stony Man Farm as the guest of Mr. Hal Brognola. Dress: casual. R.S.V.P.: not necessary.

Katz had received the puzzling summons while engaged in the Middle East in a reconnaissance that was strictly involved with gauging the potential success of a certain future mission. He'd mused about his life then, about how he'd thought of America as his home. He'd been born of Jewish parents who'd fled to France from Russia during the Bolshevik pogrom and was the last of his entire family to survive the Nazi fanatics of World War II.

As a teenager he had fought to establish an Israel that Jews everywhere had craved for centuries. He had helped win, but he'd also left an arm there and acquired scars and wounds that would go with him into the grave.

He'd lost his wife and child, too, eventually replacing them with Phoenix Force. Stony Man Farm became the old family home, and there was no question where his loyalties lay. He had made arrangements to fly back in short order.

HAVING FLOWN at nearly Mach 2 on military aircraft, he suffered jet lag as the Harrier put him down on the short runway at the Farm's camouflaged airport.

From there he walked past the Farm's collection of rustic buildings set amid a dense hardwood and conifer forest. Beyond stretched the grassy meadows of the Blue Ridge terrain, lying under the benevolent surveillance of Stony Man Mountain, one of the highest peaks in the region.

The day of the "party" was typical, pleasantly cool with a breath of wind, and low-hanging clouds banding the mountain peak like the collar of a priest.

Inside the main building Katz crossed briskly to the conference room, which actually served as the War Room of the paramilitary Phoenix Force, as well as that of Able Team and Mack Bolan, the famed Executioner.

Admitted by a security code, Katz entered to see two of his teammates on either side of the long conference table. To his left sat Gary Manning and David McCarter. At six feet, both of them towered over his own five feet nine inches.

They were both a couple of decades younger than himself, but they wouldn't dream of calling him the "old man." Time and again they had watched him in the field where he fought as hard as any of them. In fact, the younger men often tired first.

And he had experiences, many years' worth of fighting experiences, to call upon when the battle got rough.

To his right sat the last two members of the team. Closest was Rafael Encizo. Pushing forty, he was the shortest man on the team, a survivor of Cuba's barbarian rule by Fidel Castro. Like Katz, his body was scarred by some of the world's most brutal terrorists and killers who operated from both inside and outside of established governments.

Next to him sat the kid of the outfit, twenty-nine-year-old Calvin Thomas James. He was the only man on the Force who had been born in the United States. He was also the most recent replacement and the only black.

Federal agent Hal Brognola was Stony Man's White House liaison, and he paced about impatiently while he waited to get everybody's attention.

"Katz," he said with a nod. "I'm glad you were able to get here so quickly. I was about to begin. Won't you have a chair?"

Katz nodded and settled into his unofficial position at the end of the table closest to the entry.

"I have a pleasant surprise for all of you," Brognola said with pride.

He was fondling a cigar with a loving smile. That was a good sign. When he was angry or had a mission that he dreaded to assign, the big Fed chewed unlit stogies, biting the wet, shredded ends as he completed a phase of his presentation.

"This assignment you are going to like."

Katzenelenbogen squeezed his heavy eyebrows down over his light blue eyes. He ran a hand over the top of the gray hair that made him look slightly older than he really was.

"Any mission ordered from Stony Man is not an invitation to the waltz," Katz said, not without a touch of sarcasm. He raised his prosthetic arm on the table and let it bang against the highly polished wood surface.

"Mack Bolan doesn't take vacations," Gary Manning said.

His statement was not precisely correct, but the Farm was a living legacy of Bolan, the Executioner. Bolan had dedicated his life to fight evil: the Mafia, Vietnamese Communists who still held POWs as prisoners, terrorists, and any other lethal scum that could not be scrubbed away by the slow machinery of the law.

Katz and the others in the room were an extension of Bolan's relentless crusade.

They were the Phoenix Force regulars.

The five of them were field soldiers, a sort of foreign legion that roamed the world as a minuscule invisible extension of the American military that normally protected the U.S.A. and her allies.

They were surgeons who could remove a mob of terrorists or a fanatic dictator without a massive display of military power that could ignite World War III.

"Are you trying to say you're sending us out on a holiday, old chum?" David McCarter leaned back in the casual appearance he liked to affect. The veneer masked the natural and deep suspicion he held for almost everyone. Suspicion served a professional fighter well. Today McCarter's eyes glowed with skepticism. He conceived the invitation as a trick.

"Better than a picnic." Hal Brognola continued to smile.

Gary Manning possessed a dry wit, and he ventured a guess. "You're sending us to Arabia to guard a harem of girls who are not getting enough attention from the elderly sheikh." He showed a hint of a smile.

A brilliant man with a degree in stress mechanics, Manning had a look that some people associated with the outdoorsman type. His cheekbones were high, his brows heavy, his chin square, and his front teeth displayed a somewhat unsightly gap in the middle.

He had spent much of his adult life involved in violence. One of the few Canadians to serve in Vietnam, he had been cited for bravery behind enemy lines.

Later he had been trained by West Germany's elite GSG squad for service in the Royal Canadian Mounted Police. When there were no longer enough terrorists fighting the linguistic war to keep him occupied in Canada, he had drifted into the Phoenix Force.

He liked opportunities to flirt with danger. More important, as a member of the Force he was able to satisfy an inner need. The Force gave him the opportunity to actually do something about injustice.

Mack Bolan, who had been instrumental in assembling Phoenix Force, had recognized Manning as a natural team member from their first meeting.

Manning showed the determination of an oak tree where most men bent with the wind. Most read the accounts of fanatic assaults on civilization and clucked their tongues. They thought they did enough just by abhorring the slaughter by murderers and dictators and bloody revolutionaries who only wanted to supplant the existing government with their greed for power.

That wasn't enough for Manning. He just had to do something a lot more concrete.

When the offer came to join the Force, Manning grabbed for it. When the most recent call had caught up with him, he was tired of his lodge in the Canadian bush and tired of training. Recently there had been too much time between missions, and he wasn't thrilled by the prospect of a "picnic."

Neither were the others.

Brognola shook his head. He evidently failed to understand his troops as well as he thought. "I'm serious. I'm sending you on a vacation, all expenses paid."

This time the derisive sound came from the Cuban, Rafael Encizo. A scar beneath his mouth gave him a menacing appearance that helped provide space for him at bars and other crowded gatherings.

Actually all his battle scars were covered by his clothes. He'd suffered the facial wound in a neighborhood tumble when he was a teenager. His squarish Indian face was marked by determination and confronted opponents with a tough, antagonistic look.

After his Bronx cheer, Rafael leaned back and folded his arms over his trim waistline.

The head Fed took stock of the group again, searching for an answer to an elusive puzzle. Katz, McCarter, Manning, Encizo and Calvin James. They were a powerful strike force. When not working, most of them reentered the ordinary world, but when they gathered at headquarters they were not interested in talk about vacations. They expected action.

Brognola knew that, but prolonged the game a little longer. "Now listen—I am sending you on a vacation. With a regular tour group. Guide and all. To one of the world's most unspoiled resorts."

Calvin James tried to be a wiseass. "Tierra del Fuego," he guessed.

The city he suggested claimed to be the most southerly town in the world. Only a small mountain and a few miles of ice-littered water separated it from the ice cap and the South Pole.

"No, no, no. I'm sending you to Yalta."

McCarter moved forward in his seat. Beneath the surface, he was short-tempered, and he seemed ready to lash out at what he perceived as nonsense. "Vacation in Yalta? The Russian Yalta? Come along there, governor. Square with us."

"You'll like Yalta. The locals love American tourists there, any kind of tourist who brings in the hard currency that Russia needs to buy anything from outside its satellite nations."

"Who'd be stupid enough to buy rubles?" Katz asked.

"Precisely. So with practically all of the Uncle Sam dollars you want, you'll be staying right on the beach at the Hotel International, which has hundreds of lavishly furnished rooms, a dinner theater that can hold a thousand people for one of the world's greatest floor shows on a stage bigger than we have anywhere in the country.

"And get this. A private beach with no Russians allowed except for Politburo members and top KGB officials. A mile of sand sprinkled with bikini-clad sunbathers from all over the world."

"Why would we want to share a beach with KGB officials? Still, I smell a sales pitch here," Calvin James mused as he drummed his fingers against the tabletop.

"Like the pitch Roosevelt got at Yalta more than forty years ago," Katz mused.

"What?" The younger men looked to him for an explanation.

"A bit of history," he said. "Near the end of World War II, President Roosevelt went to Yalta and ended up giving Joseph Stalin a free hand to take over Poland, Hungary, Bulgaria, Czechoslovakia. Oh, you guys are a little young to give a damn about that."

"Yes, well," Brognola returned to his subject. "About this vacation—"

"Hal, I hope this is not another of your subterfuges," McCarter interrupted.

"No. Don't thank me. It's all on the National Security Council's budget. You'll have practically every day of your vacation to do with as you want."

"Now comes the price," Gary Manning said with a prudent nod of his head.

"It's a simple task, actually. One man could do it, but I thought you men would like to vacation together for a change."

Brognola pushed a button. A large screen slid down from the ceiling, and a slide projector cast a photo on the silver fabric. Occasionally the view changed as computers extrapolated from the actual picture.

"Shot from a satellite?" Katz inquired.

"Yes."

Encizo squinted. "Looks like an innocent little town to me."

"It is." Brognola manipulated several buttons until the roof view concentrated on a small segment of the town. The viewer could distinguish cars from trucks, stores from houses. However, every structure was partially obscured by trees and brush, or roof angles left much to the imagination.

"An ordinary Russian village, but the houses don't fit the patterns we are accustomed to. Nothing ominous, mind you. Just curious details."

McCarter was impatient. "Didn't those dorks over at NSC get an angle shot?"

"Impossible. The village is surrounded by a forest of tall trees."

Katz had grown more interested. "Heat sensors, high tech stuff?"

"Everything has been tried. There is absolutely no energy source or other telltale sign that suggests this is anything more sinister than a typical Russian village."

Manning snorted impatiently. He had been called in from his wilderness cabin where he had been putting on the last touches of the A-frame roof. "Then what are we doing here, if there's nothing different about the place?"

The man at the front of the room switched slides. "Ah, but there is a difference." This time the screen showed a great expanse of forest. Even the valley where the village lay was quite heavily wooded.

"One month," Brognola said. "The boys at the White House missed the change for God knows how long. But when they got on the ball, they discovered an interesting point. The woods were thinned and every structure built within a one-month span."

Encizo shook his head. "You're saying the Russians built that entire town in thirty days."

"Yes."

"Impossible." He did not believe what he was being told.

Katz interjected a thought. "It could be a movie set, nothing but shells of buildings. All facades."

"Negative."

"Portable buildings," Calvin James suggested. "They use a lot of portable buildings at schools these days. As enrollment shifts, they can move the temporary buildings to the part of town where more classrooms are needed."

Brognola picked up a file folder and slid it down the table. He knew Katz would be the one to spend the most time studying the report.

"We can detect a normal population. The buildings have the expected mass. They are not empty shells. The photo experts claim they could detect enough furniture being brought in to furnish every residence. We've calculated the amount of food brought in. The amount of garbage trucked away. So it is a real town. Real people live there.

"But it was built and populated in thirty days."

"Why?" Encizo asked. "It could be done, of course. Bring in busloads of carpenters. Prefabricate most of the work elsewhere and assemble it on the spot. But why?"

"That's the assignment, Encizo. All you have to do is find out what the town is really like. Vacation in Yalta. Two weeks in the sun. First thing, though, one or more of you can sneak away from the group and take a jaunt. The village is only twenty miles from your hotel. Have a look, see if there is anything unusual about the place that does not show up on our satellite pictures."

"And?" Katz asked.

"And nothing. Well, there is a sense of urgency."

"I knew it," Katz said.

"Yeah, now comes the problem," Manning said.

"It doesn't constitute a problem. It's just... well, there was this kid CIA agent. He was supposed to look at the place since he was in that area, anyway."

"It's just that he never came back," Encizo suggested.

"Yes, that's meaningful in itself, but there is something else that's important. It was the last message he sent. He said there was great urgency that we... Well, that's the problem, see. His message was fragmented. Apparently he tried to tell us about the town, but all that came through was that it was urgent, a matter of days."

"What was urgent?" Katz asked.

"That's what I just told you. He saw or learned something about the town or the people and tried to tell us we had only a couple of days to react. The kid was a little too deep into cloak-and-dagger stuff. But the President wants it checked out. And he doesn't want the CIA involved. If a second CIA man got caught in that area, it would embarrass the President. We're not closely linked to the White House, so he wants us to have a look, in a hurry, like right now. Is that clear?"

Katz said slowly, "I suppose. I just don't understand the urgency."

"The President of the United States will be in Venice, Italy, next week to greet the most brilliant computer experts in the free world who are now making a goodwill appearance in Russia—"

"A show-off appearance, I would say," McCarter interrupted. "If America was not so far ahead of the Communists in the computer field, we couldn't hope to defend ourselves."

"Yes, well, they will be giving Russian experts a few scraps of way-out computerese to show good faith.

Then they sail for Venice and their climax with the President."

"Climax with the President?" Encizo picked up on the double meaning.

Brognola was not amused. "Not funny."

"Yes, sir, Mr. Brognola."

"At the village, you look. You don't take pictures. You don't call me on some line you think is safe. You don't carry any weapons."

"No weapons?" Manning and McCarter spoke in unison.

"Absolutely no weapons, no matter how well you think they are concealed. And that goes for the gun barrel you use in your mechanical arm, Katz. The mission does not warrant taking any unnecessary chances. If you're taken into custody, the worst they can say is that you didn't stay with your Intourist guide. The Russians won't scare off other tourists for a minor breach of that nature. And your papers are perfect. Unless you pull something stupid like arming yourselves with poison darts, you will be dealt with at the local level where you will never be connected to Phoenix Force."

"And we don't call you when we've seen the town?" Katz asked for reassurance.

"Absolutely no calls unless it's a doomsday warning. The mission is not critical. I'll debrief you upon your return. Does everyone understand? You peek at the town. Then you enjoy your vacation. Follow orders and absolutely nothing can go wrong."

James shrugged his shoulders. "That seems easy enough. How about you guys?"

"Yeah, I guess," Encizo replied, but he seemed troubled.

"Manning?" Brognola asked.

"Yes."

"McCarter?"

"I love a mystery. A little town springs up almost overnight. Sounds intriguing."

"Katz."

"Why does this seem too simple?" Yakov Katzenelenbogen said.

"Because you're accustomed to intrigue, boxes inside of boxes. That's why this is exactly what this team needs. An easy assignment for a change."

Katz leaned back in his chair. He entwined his fingers behind the back of his neck and stared at the slide on the screen.

"Too simple," he said.

"Ah, Katz." Encizo started to look forward to the vacation. "What can happen?"

"I can't think of a single problem."

"See, you admit it."

"It's when I can't foresee the problems that I worry."

"Relax," Brognola told him.

Katz finally stopped bringing up his concerns. He sensed danger in anything he did not understand, but he couldn't refuse a mission simply because he was at a loss to come up with a reason for objecting.

Later, when he could be alone, he would go through mental gyrations to look for a trap. But in the end he would quietly agree and fly Pan-Am like any vacationer.

UP TO THEIR PRESENT predicament, nothing had gone wrong.

But now, as he stood on the edge of the woods overlooking the town, Katz glanced from one corpse to another and wished he had dug deeper before they had left the States.

He no longer believed there was anything innocent about the town they had come to see and knew that Phoenix Force was in a tight fix.

Katz gave a mournful nod of his head. "Vacation?" he asked of no one in particular, then turned away from the bodies and stepped from the woods.

3

Stoically, Katz dragged the last body deeper into the forest while Gary Manning and David McCarter covered the tracks. They sacrificed the advantages of burying or covering the dead in favor of time.

Finished, they stood bathed in the glowing sunset, contemplating their next move.

"A picnic," Gary Manning mumbled. "Like picnicking with a pack of grizzly bears."

McCarter bitched, too. "Brognola called it a holiday. Gotta be Argus-eyed just to survive this vacation. Five dead, and God knows what happens when the police or the KGB stumble across our trail."

Katz remained silent. Once more he recalled what the head Fed had said back at Stony Man Farm and what he had stated to be their objectives.

Take a look at the town and come home. Nothing more.

"We ought to go back to the hotel in Yalta," he said.

"Go back!" McCarter sounded appalled. "We don't know enough to call it quits. I mean this is weird. Look." He pointed to bright lights near the edge of town closest to them. "Exxon, and it's even self-service."

"McDonald's." Gary Manning nodded toward the familiar arch. "And over there, A & P. I mean, the

Russians could use some supermarkets. They'd freak out if they saw shelves filled with everything from Wheaties to caviar. Probably think it was a KGB trick. But an A & P store here, that's as queer as moose seducing a bear."

"It's a scene from a science-fiction video," Katz said. "We've stepped through a time warp."

Manning nodded in agreement.

"Then we go closer," the Briton said. "Must take a better look at this oddity, or I'll think I'm hallucinating."

Manning agreed, but Katz still vacillated. "It's against orders," he finally said.

"To hell with the orders. Brognola wouldn't want us to quit if he knew what we're looking at."

"The guys at the hotel might get edgy when we don't return in time."

McCarter became impatient. "They wouldn't go back if they were here, looking through our eyes."

Katz tried to weigh their chances. "You know Encizo and James. If we're not back on schedule, they're going to come looking for us. The question is, do we risk their lives so we can satisfy our curiosity?"

Silence greeted his words as the two men weighed the issues.

"Maybe you're right," Manning conceded. "Figuring this place out isn't worth disobeying orders or risking our lives. Hell, we could end up getting ourselves into a real trapper's stew if we hang around much longer."

His tone had changed. He sounded like a man anxious to avoid getting "involved."

But then he rarely presented a clear-cut picture of himself. He looked like a man who loved a quiet lake, its surface broken by a muskie fiercely clamping its jaws around an artificial lure. He could be mistaken for a rugged, reclusive deer hunter, but no one would guess that in Canada he hunted game for food and anywhere around the globe he hunted men as food for his obsessive desire to thin the herd of human predators.

"You two go back," Katz said suddenly.

His associates had anticipated that decision. They understood Katz. They knew his story. Somebody who had sustained a lot of personal losses was willing to take more chances with his safety.

They suspected he would give up his life without regret—if the price, the cause was right. Phoenix Force provided the perfect solution to the dilemma of a man who had limited reasons to live. He would take on assignments until he finally died in action, having taken with him scores of the world's assorted monsters.

Manning and McCarter exchanged negative looks that let Katz know they did not find his plan agreeable.

"We should return to the States and report what we've found. This place is too peaceful. Too innocent looking. There's none of the barbed wire or guard towers you'd expect at a Russian installation, but there has got to be more to it than what's visible."

"There were five armed guards," Manning reminded him.

"Five guards patrolling together? We haven't seen any other security men."

"So?"

"So they didn't expect any problems or..."

"Or they were hunters, carrying weapons you'd never see regular security men using," McCarter said.

"Five buddies out shooting rabbits. And we killed them."

"It won't wash," Manning said. "They spoke English. They got uptight when Katz used Russian. They were guards, all right. Poor ones, maybe, but they weren't out shooting cottontails."

"Look," Katz said. "One man can handle this. Besides, I've got a premonition. The deal is too simple. This is the kind of mission that could end in disaster."

It was an eerie, mysterious kind of place, so inviting that it could be his downfall. He hated to take the others with him, but he knew they would not let him proceed alone.

"Okay," he said. "We go in. Just stroll in like we were three buddies or three guards coming in off the line at the end of the shift."

"Walk straight in?" Manning blinked with surprise.

"Yes. Or you two can cover me."

"No," McCarter said. "I like the idea. We go in straight and see as much as we can. The place is too big for everyone to know everyone else."

Manning grumbled. "I don't like it, but I'm outvoted. So let's go."

Before they could step off, an unexpected sound, familiar and reassuring, made them pause.

A church bell was ringing at the end of the town's main street.

THE REVEREND ARNOLD VULCAN beamed from the pulpit at the front of the small church.

"May the Good Lord shine his light upon you."

He finished his brief sermon with the usual satisfaction. He appreciated the irony. Arnold Vulcan, the hardline Communist playing the role of born-again Christian. He loved wearing a false face. Every night, every day was a costume party.

And he was the devil incarnate.

Every day he grew stronger in his role and secretly hoped he was becoming indispensable to the state.

With a well-practiced semblance of intimacy, he leaned forward so his elbows were on the podium and his fingers curved over the front of the gleaming wood.

"Friends, and I do think of you all—" He interrupted himself because he was an avowed perfectionist, and no error could go uncorrected. "'You all' is a Southern expression. Only those designated as living below the Mason-Dixon line will ever use it. Now, as I was saying, friends, God has favored us with a marvelous opportunity."

Hiding his cynicism of religion was not easy, but he worked hard at it.

He had spent all of his forty years of life, except for his early childhood days, climbing a political ladder that he had built in his mind. The ladder's feet were planted solidly in the earth of Party doctrine. The lower steps had meant fervent, dedicated service to the Communist youth movement. He'd openly campaigned for leadership.

His application for the KGB was filed the moment he was old enough to be eligible. He took a stint in "Wet Work." Whenever possible, he had personally handled interrogations and was adept at torture. This blood sport gave him an aura of toughness that frightened the less dedicated men in the organization.

But he had connived his way out of the sadistic realm and skipped to pure espionage as quickly as possible. He had sought assignments in the United States and again proved his faith by pretending he was eager to return home when ordered. No one ever thought he would defect. And he would not. Only in Russia could he gain power—pure, raw, vicious power over others.

Power was his bread. Brutality was his wine.

He had risen quickly through the ranks, but now he wanted to move out of the KGB and into a spotlight of his own. Although national leaders frequently had covert action experience in their background, he had sensed early that the new realm was slyly demoting both the intelligence and military organizations.

Here in Cheyenne, a city of his own making, he was not only building a name and a reputation, but he was also carving a tight little niche for himself.

The "Reverend" Arnold Vulcan worked directly for the Politburo. He had been so successful with his individual projects that the men who ran the vast empire gathered Cheyenne to their own protective arms.

If the current project succeeded, he had no doubt he would either move directly into the ruling council or at least have his name at the top of the waiting list.

All he would have to do for such a giant leap forward was to hint that he had another idea with equal potential.

The Reverend Vulcan would stop at nothing to make the Cheyenne project a masterful success. Many would die in the process. Sacrifices, human sacrifices would be necessary. But he considered the victims martyrs who would elevate him to a point where he could provide a better living for his people, where he could expand the empire, where he could exert control.

He was the chosen one.

"Those invited here tonight for this brief but all-important fellowship meeting have been given a mission."

He prided himself on working religion into every pronouncement about this mission. It was a disarming asset to be considered a cleric when he worked abroad.

Surprisingly the elation he had expected from his audience came back to him as a buzz of nervous tension.

"Did you not hear me?"

Vulcan allowed an inkling of threat to coax his "parishioners."

Neither Vulcan nor Arnold was his real name, of course, but he expected to continue using them. Vulcan, like Alexander the Great, was a name suited for historic leaders.

Within five years he would be in the Politburo, he promised himself. The world would need him there by then.

"I say again." He raised his voice. "Did you hear me? Jesus Christ, Our Savior, has deemed us fit to serve His cause. Hallelujah."

A tall, powerful man wearing jeans and a T-shirt with an I Love New York inscription stood at the rear of the church. He went by the name of Ollie Larson-Swenson. A native-born American according to his passport, he did not affect an accent.

"All this religious garbage offends me," he said. "I am a good Party member."

"The phony cloak of religion will not offend you when you are confronted by inquisitive CIA bastards."

"It is not only the religious trash," Larson continued. "It's the mission. We are not ready." He lapsed into Russian, as though the English failed to convey his feelings on the matter.

"English! English! English!" Vulcan raged.

A tall, strong man with gray at his temples and piercing blue eyes, Vulcan rarely lost control. He was like steel, and the flames around him were no more danger to him than the heat of a match.

"We heard that we will be used as assassins in the United States," a woman said. "Doesn't the KGB have a section of trained killers?"

"Morkrie Dela," a man said. "Why should we do their work?"

"There is no *Morkrie Dela*. You were not sent here to become mere assassins, but you will do as you are ordered, wherever you are. And if I hear one more word of Russian spoken from this moment until our triumphant return, I will have the individual and his entire family deported to Siberia. Understood?"

No one answered.

"Good. Now return to your homes and pack. Only the items on your personal list. Your travel guides will inspect your luggage. There must be no links between you and the motherland."

"Are you saying we will be leaving tomorrow, comrade?"

"Comrade? You idiot. I should have you—" Just then Vulcan was interrupted by a boy who entered from the wings and who proceeded to inform him in a whisper that five guards had not reported in on time.

Vulcan wasn't concerned. "Probably drunk somewhere," he said.

The security men were cadre. While they lived the American way, they were not sent on long-term missions. And they had little to do. No one had ever attempted to enter the town.

"Send out a posse to find them and bring them to me."

The boy assumed a puzzled expression at that command.

"Posse means a group of men sent out to search for an outlaw. Haven't you been watching the films as required?"

"Yes, pastor, I will form a posse right away."

With him, Vulcan could pretend to have forgotten Larson's breaches of policy. He smiled broadly, sending a benevolent look at the youngster.

"Express your excitement. How often do you get a chance to live the materialistic life-style of the decadent West?"

"How long will we live to enjoy this opportunity," Larson persisted, "if we are sent on a particularly dangerous assignment before we are ready?"

There were murmurs of support all around. A few, those designated as born-again Christians, stayed in their roles even as they questioned Vulcan's wisdom.

"Jesus would not call upon us so soon."

"Christ cannot protect against our own lack of training."

"Besides," Larson said, "those who have gone before us had one long-term assignment alone, a man and wife at most. We are being sent in a herd, like cattle. Surely it is more hazardous."

"There is safety in numbers."

"Like hell."

"Amen."

"I say 'amen' to that, too."

"So do I."

"Think of being awarded the Order of the Red Flag," Vulcan told them. "Even the Gold Star is possible."

Larson attacked again.

"We want to know the nature of this mission."

"It is a great pilgrimage. A real blow for communism. You will be given details en route."

"You want us to go now?"

"Impossible. Unwise."

Larson drew himself up. "Unless we know the mission, it is impossible for us to go."

A silence gripped the chamber.

Mutiny. That could not be allowed, and Vulcan knew the remedy. He took a pen and small notebook from his pocket. Even before he scribbled with the pen, the silence developed into a dead stillness.

To make the arrogant humble themselves before him brought Vulcan a gratification that was almost sexual. People were sheep, he thought. A lone wolf could attack the flock, knowing that no others would band together against him.

Larson growled with contempt for his timid cohorts. "Ah, you are all fish. You would swim into the shark's mouth for fear of his teeth." He stalked from the church, spreading both doors as if a vast space was needed for his great bulk to pass through.

In a way Vulcan admired the big man. Too bad he would have to die in his own explosion, lest he be traced back to the Soviet Union.

But few from his "parish" would return, Vulcan knew. He had already commenced a list of those marked for death.

The congregation waited for permission to leave.

"Go. Make ready for what we have practiced. The order to move out may come any day, any hour. With luck we will have some days to shop in the West."

The promise of shopping in a non-Communist nation cheered the phony worshipers, and they left, joking and laughing.

Only one young woman remained.

She was thirty-two and had never been married, according to her dossier. It was difficult to understand why she had not been pursued by many men.

She was beautiful. Tall, five-eight or more without the heels that emphasized the taut, graceful muscles of her legs. Hers was a body fitting the universal standard of perfection. More than adequate breasts, slim waist and perfectly shaped hips. She was dressed like an American businesswoman and wore horn-rimmed glasses that could not detract from the sensuousness in her deep blue eyes. She had an inviting mouth, clear tanned skin, and her long, light brown hair gleamed with highlights.

He had never wanted to screw any other woman so badly, but he was certain that she was a KGB agent paid to watch his every move. He must be careful.

"Ah, yes, my dear Anna. My dear, dear, Anna."

She had been gone briefly, to Moscow for instruction, he supposed. Seeing her after the brief absence gave him an excuse to kiss her in greeting, but when he tried she turned her cheek. He pretended that she had only meant to protect her makeup, so his lips touched the back of her neck near her hairline.

"Ann Cardwell," she said coyly. "Anna is a name for milkmaids in America."

"They have no women milking cows in the United States," he instructed her. "They use only machines, so the women must live on the streets and serve as low-priced whores. But let us go celebrate."

"I must go pack if we are leaving so soon."

"If you do not come to my quarters, I could have your name dropped from the list," he threatened. He could not know with any certainty, but he guessed she wanted nothing more than to get out of the USSR.

"You do not have such power as yet, Comrade Colonel," she said.

"I will have such power soon," he insisted.

"Invite me then."

He ran his tongue across his lips. Next to power, she was the thing he wanted most. The pleasure of having her would be doubly delicious because she would detest every minute of it.

Not waiting for him to say anything, she walked away from him and out into the cool evening.

He stood in the church doorway, looking after her with a gleam in his eyes, then turning his attention to and admiring his city.

"Genius," he told himself. "Sheer genius."

4

Katz could almost smell the danger. He had no doubts that the town existed for a sinister purpose.

He knew the Russian mentality, or at least, that of the Communist dictators who ran the prison empire. Even the current "enlightened" rulers who decreed incentives and toyed with supposedly freer elections were men of unfailing determination. Katz suspected that they would never relinquish any significant power to the people. The subjects of autocrats had a way of turning on their masters when the reins were loosened.

Those in the Party extended that caution to the international scene. They knew empires continued to gobble up colonies or the colonials became restless. As long as the Russian sphere of influence, besides the occupied satellite countries, continued to grow, there was not much hope of pushing back the Iron Curtain. People, like gamblers, bet on players with a winning streak.

And the USSR was not likely to build a fantasyland or theme park like Cheyenne that flaunted capitalist prosperity. Besides, in the two hours since they had first spotted the bizarre village, no one had entered or left. The road in had remained empty.

But downtown buzzed with activity. People entered and left the assortment of stores. They drove late-model American and Japanese cars from the business area to the residential sections. Several disappeared inside the church.

But there was no sound. The distance and trees muffled the usual noise.

Pantomime, Katz thought. Television without sound.

Strange. He had felt more competent dealing with the five guards. Silence was an ambush waiting for the unwary.

He knew he should scout from all points on the compass, but time was limited. He wanted to be back in Yalta before James and Encizo came looking for them.

Manning pressed for action. "Well, are we going in or aren't we?"

They stood in the graying darkness. In the west the sun had left behind a narrow slash of crimson tinsel.

"Memorize the layout of the streets," Katz said. His tone had betrayed concern.

"The service station is the first thing on the right," Manning thought aloud. "New and used car lot next door. Looks as though it holds one of every make and model they could get."

"ROP near the end of the streets," McCarter remarked.

"ROP?" Katz repeated, not understanding.

"Regional Occupations Program," McCarter explained. "It's big back home. A kid gets out of high school and finds the only thing he knows is Shakespeare and the bones of a crawdad. He goes to an ROP center to learn accounting, computer, drafting; in other words, how to make a living."

"Oh."

"McDonald's on the left." McCarter noted. "What do you think of stopping there first? Guards coming in from their shift might drop in there."

Manning disagreed. "More likely they'd stop at the Ox Bow Tavern next door."

"We'll stop at McDonald's," said Katz. "In a dark bar we might come up against a herd of drinkers whose eyes are already dilated. So what else do we have, Gary?"

"Got a jewelry store, drugstore, a multiscreen theater beyond the tavern. The rest seem to be dress shops, shoe stores, a giant ComputerLand, and the church."

"Supermarket on the right and—" McCarter whistled in surprise "—do my eyes deceive me or is that a gun store?"

"We take that early on, if we have to," Katz responded. "The second there's shooting or the minute it looks dangerous, we take the gun shop. We commandeer everything we can carry."

"What's the strategy? Are we going to shoot up the bloody town?"

"It depends upon what happens. Our best bet is to take a look and get out so we can get word back. In any case, fighting is a last resort."

"Then what about an escape route?"

Katz shook his head. "I don't know. How about you, McCarter? How long does it take you to hot-wire a car?"

"Quicker than it takes a Scotsman to put a penny in his purse. But if this recon patrol takes long, James and Encizo will already be on the road. How do we keep them from coming after us?"

Katz looked at McCarter. "Planning an escape is a job for you. Agreed?"

"Yeah, I'll set—"

Manning interrupted. "Look, there are more people entering the church."

As they looked on, a few people parked in the lot at the side of the church while more approached from the residential areas on foot.

"Do we wait?" Manning asked.

Katz shook his head. "People in the street will make us less conspicuous unless someone has a way of knowing we're not the real security troops."

"Then this is it?"

"Yes, let's move out. Carry the guns as casually as a bunch of hunters."

They moved like footsore men, chatting among themselves with a casual air.

Manning weighed the odds as they walked. "Damn, we've taken on some big forces before," he thought aloud. "But I can't remember taking on an entire town."

Neither of the others replied. The closer they came to the brightly lit service station, the more intent they became.

Katz was mulling over a disturbing concept. From experience he could not imagine the Russians building an idyllic village for any other purpose than to satisfy some militaristic need. Over much of the world it was unfortunately true that cannons came before groceries.

Then his philosophical thoughts gave way to the demands of reality as they arrived at McDonald's. Katz opened the door and held it as his partners entered.

The place was bright, well kept and empty. Sounds came from the kitchen, the voices of a young male and a young female.

The girl whose voice they had heard appeared quickly. She was bright-eyed with a fresh clean look about her.

"May I help, gentlemen?" she asked in English with an enticing smile, apparently not finding it unusual that they carried guns.

"Three burgers and three chocolate shakes," Katz ordered for all of them, and let a bare suggestion of an accent salt his speech.

"Shakes?" The girl cocked her head, as though she didn't understand.

"Chocolate. Three of them."

"Oh." She nodded comprehendingly. "You mean milk shakes."

"Yes. Isn't that what I said?"

"No. You just said 'shakes.' In America they're called milk shakes. A mistake like that could blow your cover."

Katz absorbed that bit of mistaken information.

She called the order to the back room and leaned her elbows on the counter. "Business is slow when a class is about to graduate."

"Really?"

She finally appeared to notice the guns.

"You're new in Cheyenne, aren't you?"

"Yes," Manning responded.

"How long?"

"*Aboot* a week," Manning replied.

The girl picked up immediately on the pronunciation of "about."

"Oh, dear, that's not the way the Americans say 'about.' They'd guess in a second that you were Canadian. Maybe Scotch. I do hope you're not scheduled for a mission soon."

"Mission?" McCarter said, and mentally Katz flinched at the younger man's blunder.

"Yes. Mission. You know about missions, don't you?" Her turquoise eyes clouded.

Any more mistakes, and they would expose themselves, Katz thought worriedly.

"Three burgers and three milk shakes," a slender teenager called out as he came around from the back room. The burgers were wrapped in paper, more like fish and chips than the American penchant for using plastic boxes.

Katz grew skeptical of how far the pretence was carried as he came to the conclusion that the sandwiches could not have been prepared from scratch in the short time they had been in the shop.

"That'll be twenty-two dollars and fifty-five cents," the girl said pleasantly.

Manning bristled and dug for his wallet.

When he handed across the money, the girl took it and laughed. "You flunked again. Hamburgers and milk shakes don't cost that much. You have a lot to learn."

The boy appeared concerned rather than amused. "Are you three cadre?"

Katz stepped in before his friends could speak. Cadre. He knew what he meant. If they were cadre, they would remain for some time to direct those enrolled in training.

"Yes. You're really alert."

"We're cadre, too," the girl said, "but the Reverend Vulcan has promised we'll be sent on a mission soon. Probably to the real Cheyenne. The Strategic Missile Wing is there, and Reverend Vulcan is always sending new people in hopes of getting more of us employed at the base. But that's not the emphasis now, of course."

Katz now had a handle on the entire operation. They were in the midst of an elaborate base for training espionage agents who would blend easily into the American society. How many had graduated already? he wondered.

"I'm aware of that," Katz bluffed. "But has he announced a time?"

"Tonight maybe. Tomorrow at the latest. That's what everyone is guessing. Must be ten or twenty people going."

"You sure they're heading for the real Cheyenne?"

"I didn't say that."

The boy turned to her. "You know you can't answer a question like that, Sis."

"How could I know where they're going for sure?" she said, trying to backpedal.

Katz tensed, knowing that things had gotten awkward.

The boy looked suspicious. "You guys should know it's forbidden to gossip about such subjects."

"Yes." The girl's hands shook. "You aren't testing us, I hope."

The boy put an arm around her. "I think we should call in Reverend Vulcan."

Katz felt the first real prickle of danger and tried to salvage the situation.

"We're security guards. Nobody tells us anything."

McCarter tried to help. "All we do is walk through the woods until we're relieved." He used his language skills to sound like an American.

"Where are the other two?" the boy asked. "The guards always come in together."

Katz covered that one. "They went next door to get a drink. I hope that isn't against the rules."

"How long did you say you've been in town?"

"Came in last week," Manning said.

"I meet everybody who gets off the bus. Hand out coffee and doughnuts. But you should know that," the boy said, and for a moment, the three guns began rising.

The kid's wise to us, Katz thought.

"They must have brought you in by truck."

"Right. By truck."

"Nice to have you with us." The boy's voice wavered, and Katz realized that the team was no longer fooling the young cook. "If you'll excuse me, I see the church service is starting. I'd better get ready. Reverend Vulcan's sermons whet the appetite, as the Americans say."

Katz looked through the window. The street no longer buzzed with people. Most of those who remained in sight were headed for the church, except for a lone woman who walked in the opposite direction from the crowd and was rapidly approaching the fast-food outlet.

A door opened and closed quietly in the rear of the restaurant, and to Katz's ear, alert for danger, the closing door was as loud as a klaxon. He wasted no time in committing the team to action. "Get the boy," he ordered.

McCarter rounded the counter and rushed past the girl. Manning charged through the front exit and around the side of the building.

"What's happening?" the girl cried, then sucked in her breath in an instinctive preface to a scream.

Katz lowered the barrel of the rifle until it pointed in the area of her heart.

She did not scream nor exhale.

The Israeli's voice was calm and very forceful, with a deadly edge to it.

"Please. Don't make me kill you."

For two or three seconds he felt she was going to cooperate.

From the street came the unmistakable sounds of violent struggles. A fist crunching into a jawbone. A sharp cry of pain. A rifle butt popping a skull as if it were a nutshell. Manning or McCarter had caught the cook.

The girl lost control, but before she could scream, Katz grasped her hair and slammed her forehead to the counter.

She slid away inertly, one arm dragging the milk shakes with her.

It was better than killing her, Katz thought. He vaulted the counter and stuffed the napkins into her mouth before stripping her belt from her waist to improvise a set of handcuffs that would hold her to a work bench.

At best, though, the Phoenix Force team had gained no more than seconds by securing the cook and the girl.

The woman outside was still approaching the restaurant, and Katz accepted the preordained outcome.

Phoenix Force would not leave town without more bloodshed—if they left at all.

5

She'd come through the door breezily, noticed Katz and glanced at the prosthetic hand with no apparent discomfort. Katz had known women who were made uncomfortable by the least suggestion of a handicap or infirmity.

It had been quite some time since he had seen someone as beautiful as the stately goddess who came through the door, and even under the pressing circumstances, she had quite an impact on him.

Tall—five foot eight, he guessed—she had a mouth that made him think of kissing, a thought that came less frequently to Katz in recent years, and she had an effortlessly sensuous look about her without even trying.

"Oh, they're looking for you," she said without any preludes.

"What?" he asked, surprised that she should speak to him as though she knew of him. She, too, spoke flawless English, American-style, which still seemed so strange to him.

His muscles were all taut, and he knew that he could be given away at any moment because the girl's prone body was visible if anyone stepped close enough to the cash register.

"There's a posse looking for you," the beautiful woman said. "When none of you reported on time, Reverend Vulcan dispatched a dozen men to search the forest." She cocked her head, and Katz couldn't help but notice the highlights in her hair. "You're new here, aren't you? I don't believe we've met."

She extended her hand, and during the handshake gazed into his eyes, making him reflect fleetingly that he would have liked to have met her under vastly different circumstances.

"Ann Cardwell," she introduced herself. "I'm Reverend Vulcan's assistant here at Cheyenne. And you?"

"Me?"

She smiled. Evidently she was accustomed to men becoming tongue-tied when they first met her.

"Oh, Dwayne Fredericks," he responded, using the phony name on his passport. "I arrived several weeks ago."

"Really? I meet all the newcomers. I'm surprised I don't remember you."

"You really mean this," he said, holding up his bad arm. "Usually I wear a replacement that's hard to distinguish from the real thing."

"That's not what I meant. You have the type of face that's difficult to forget. But what about the other guards?"

He shrugged.

"I don't know. I came in alone. There didn't seem to be much to do out there in the woods."

"There never is. Well, I'd better call Vulcan and tell him that we have at least one of you home safely." She started for the passageway to the rear of the counter, but he stepped in front of her. She tried to step around him. "There's a phone here," she said. Then she called, "Sis. Where are you?"

"Who's Sis?" He was trying to hold her up, stalling for time, but the situation was rapidly becoming more complicated. Three couples, evidently from the church, were about to enter.

"The girl who works here on this shift. She'll be shipping out for the States soon." The woman called out again, "Sis!"

Katz heard the rear door open and hoped that it was Manning and McCarter returning.

"Excuse me," Ann Cardwell said again. Then, judging by an expression on her face that she couldn't quite conceal, she spotted something behind the counter. There was no question that she had seen enough to sense trouble. "Oh. I guess Sis isn't here."

"Wait--" Katz reached for her arm and missed. The door had opened and admitted new customers who had come between her and Katz.

Manning and McCarter entered from the kitchen, and it was obvious they had taken part in a tussle.

Ann Cardwell sensed more danger, whirled and plunged into the incoming group. Although they tried to get out of her way, they threw her off her stride, and she was staggering before she reached the door.

"Don't shoot," he called to his teammates as he started after her. If he could stop her before she sounded the alarm, the team would have a better chance of escaping.

A shot would alert everyone within blocks.

"Out of my way," he yelled.

He plunged after her, shouting at the newcomers. "Stop her," he told them. "We're police. She's an agent."

A female observer believed him and clutched the escaping woman's shoulder.

The Cardwell woman lashed out with a karate chop that came close to breaking bones.

Another arm clutched her, and for a moment Katz thought he could catch her before she reached the street, but she tore free and slammed against the door.

"Not me, you fools. Them. They're CIA."

The people couldn't make up their minds about whom to believe, and they split into two segments. The women tried to follow Ann Cardwell in her escape. The men stayed to fight.

The Phoenix Force members swung into action. Katz made an upward sweeping motion with the butt of his rifle in the direction of the nearest man, but the Russian was no novice. He had raised a leg to protect his vitals and swung like a baseball pitcher with one foot hiked toward his chin. Had he landed a punch on Katz's chin, the resistance would have steadied him until he could lower his defensive leg and regain balance.

The strategy failed. Katz let the fist fan his cheek, and his opponent went rattling through tables and chairs before he hit the floor.

Katz wanted to take him out permanently, but four others were plunging toward him. In his peripheral vision he saw Manning and McCarter raising their rifles to fire.

"Not yet," he called out.

The other two obeyed, although neither understood his order. Instead they vaulted the counter while Katz absorbed the consequences of his decision to delay gunfire.

A fist cannonballed into his belly and ricocheted off his hardened muscles. He leveraged the rifle butt for a jab at the other opponent, but he was too late to deflect the finger jabbed into his left eye.

Another blow followed in short order from his blinded side. Katz staggered, hit by a double-handed clout that struck him with sledgehammer force.

As his left hip was numbed with a place kick, karate-style, Katz felt himself faltering.

Then the cavalry charged in the form of Gary Manning and David McCarter.

Katz could see the cool competence in Manning's dark gray eyes. The Canadian's deliberate grace was a deception that concealed dazzling speed as he rammed the rifle muzzle bayonet-style into the back of a Red who was preparing to lasso his chief with a garroting wire.

The muzzle shattered the spinal column, and the burly Russian crumpled to the ground helplessly.

"Strike one," Gary called.

"Make that two," McCarter yelled. He brought his heel down sideways across another man's Achilles tendon. In the same action, he smashed his rifle butt to the back of the man's knee. He slumped at the floor, his hand still clasping the back of Katz's belt. Using a balled fist carefully aimed and swung with the momentum that began above head level, McCarter hit the hand precisely where it joined the fingers.

The joints broke with the sound of breaking pretzels. From the floor, the man, now on his back, aimed a kick at McCarter's shin.

The pain destroyed his easy demeanor and activated his short temper. He delivered an abrupt and powerful blow with the rifle butt that finished the man off with a crunch of vertebrae in the neck.

"McCarter," Katz yelled. "Give me a hand."

The Englishman assessed the situation immediately. One man was locked in combat with Manning, but two others were cornering Katz, using slow, professional probes with switchblade knives. In a cramped corner of the room, Katz could evade them only so long.

"Got 'em, mate," he said as he raised his rifle.

"No. No, shooting," Katz repeated even as the point of a knife made a slit in his shirt not far from the heart.

The feisty Israeli had taken the proper defense. He squeezed the enemy's wrist between his left arm and the left side of his torso. But the move also froze him in position and the second knife wielder grinned, smelling the kill.

McCarter leaped in, raised his rifle over his head with both hands, and brought it down in front of the enemy's face, down to the Adam's apple area, and hauled back fast and hard.

The man grunted and gagged, trying to twist his knife into McCarter's flesh. The urgent need to breathe, though, proved to be his undoing, and he dropped his knife in an attempt to push the rifle away from his neck.

In the time it took the man to die, Katz dropped his rifle and used the hooks of his prosthetic device to worry his other adversary's eye, and took advantage of that distraction to sink the man's own knife into his chest and hold it there until the twitching stopped.

Now there was time to look around.

They were the only ones standing, and they were standing in the center of an open graveyard.

They wasted only seconds checking their own wounds.

"Why didn't you let us shoot them?" McCarter challenged.

"Explanations later," Katz said. "The women are escaping."

They dashed into the street. The women had reached cover inside several buildings, but one tall figure was seen racing toward the church.

It was Ann Cardwell, the beautiful woman who had greeted him pleasantly inside the restaurant. She was obviously rushing to sound the warning.

Gary Manning lifted his rifle. He would never miss at that range. The woman was not even crouching or dodging.

Katz imagined that beautiful body lying on the pavement face down in her own blood.

Manning's rifle settled on a bead.

With a quick motion Katz batted the barrel down.

Manning was surprised. "Hey, she's going to sound the alarm. We'll have the entire town down on us."

"Nothing will bring people into the streets faster than a rifle shot," Katz said.

"Okay, then what do we do?"

"Take the gun shop for now," Katz said.

A moment later Katz provided cover while Manning and McCarter burst into the gun store. It was brightly lit inside.

A clerk smiled at them from behind the counter. "Good evening, gentlemen," he said with a saccharine smile.

Manning barely raised his rifle. He fired from the hip, and a black hole opened in the clerk's forehead, and a deeply shocked look appeared on his face.

McCarter frowned at his friend, not understanding why Manning had fired in violation of Katz's orders.

To satisfy himself, McCarter leaped the counter while the clerk was sliding to the floor. The dead man's hand clenched a Colt Python that he had nearly freed of its holster.

"I saw him make his move," Gary Manning said.

"Good thing you did."

As a precaution McCarter took the long-barreled .357 Magnum and tossed it across the room. Dead men sometimes were not as dead as they looked.

"He should have used a snubnosed piece," Gary commented dryly. "He might have cleared the holster in time."

Then they took a good look around them, at the unexpected bounty, and realized that they had just run into a speck of good luck in the midst of their difficult situation.

"We've hit a bloody gold mine," McCarter said.

"The mother lode," Manning agreed.

The shop was an arsenal. Handguns hid one wall, everything from Fred Adolph's Gem, a single-shot, long-range .22 designed and built as early as 1910, to an Uzi pistol adapted for full automatic fire with a 32-round magazine of 9 mm parabellum shells.

Manning used his rifle butt to shatter the glass in the protective case and grabbed the Uzi.

Outside, the church bell clanged with angry urgency.

"So much for stealth." McCarter picked another wall display and took an FIE SPAS-12 auto assault shotgun in his left hand and, dropping his rifle, reached with his right hand for the closest thing he could reach, a 32-shot Demo TAC-1M carbine. The weight surprised him. "Hey, this thing is already loaded."

"Everything is loaded," Manning said. He rushed to the front of the store. "And everything possible has been made full automatic. They must have been expecting a full-scale war."

Manning had just reached the window when he heard a shot, then another and another.

He saw Katz retreating to the store with a mob of unarmed Russians charging after him. With every shot, one of the men flew backward or doubled over with a tunnel that a bullet had cut through his guts. Just outside the door, a burly stevedore type grabbed Katz by the arm.

Manning fired a 3-round burst from the Uzi pistol. The window exploded. Shards of glass bloodied the men behind Katz, blinding some of them. The bullets found yielding flesh, and the restraining hand dropped away from Katz's sleeve.

It was a close shot Manning had not wanted to make.

Katz whirled toward the shop, and the mob, undaunted, leaped at him. Several pairs of hands reached out, clutched and held him like an insect on flypaper.

"Hang in there, buddy," Manning yelled. He fired a longer burst that cleared a space in the crowd in a rather drastic manner.

Freed, Katz bolted across the sidewalk and dove headfirst through the gaping window frame.

He rolled across the floor, unaware of the powdered glass biting his flesh. McCarter jumped over him to provide support for Manning, who had run out of ammunition in the Uzi pistol.

Six of the locals lunged across the sidewalk in a virtual suicide attack. McCarter resisted the urge to back away. He had to stay up front to keep the enemy from reaching the safe interiors of adjoining stores.

"Number one," he yelled, turning the FIE SPAS-12 auto assault shotgun on the closest attacker.

The blast hit the man in the lower abdomen and sent him flying backward in a spiderlike dance.

McCarter then swung the gun in the direction of a tall shape sprinting toward him with track-meet speed.

The shot metamorphosed the runner into a high hurdler, then spun the man to the ground. Another of the Briton's shots blew a thin weed of a man high into the air and into the hereafter. A third dropped short of the sidewalk.

Gary Manning shouted behind McCarter, "Number three." He had taken a new .223 Bushmaster from the wall, thumbed loose the safety and fired twice.

The muzzle-flash from the short barrel was awesome. It obviously impressed still another track star hurling himself toward the Englishman.

In a desperate attempt to stop, the man flung himself onto the sidewalk and skidded through the broken glass. His head struck the bricks beneath the window. Manning leaned out easily and put a bullet through the man's brains.

"That one count?" he asked.

McCarter shook his head. "No, sitting ducks don't count, old chap."

The crowd outside had thinned with the casualties, and some of the remainder took flight while others backed away, allowing Manning and McCarter to leisurely pick them off. In so doing they inspired the survivors to greater speed.

A sudden quiet descended, and the pair tried to relax momentarily, but it was too soon.

At that moment a loud crack deafened McCarter's right ear. He whirled to see a stranger crouching in the back room. He was emptying a Czech CZ-75 at the two Phoenix Force soldiers near the front of the store, and in an attempt to kill both, he fired between them.

Katz snatched up the first gun he could reach, and in quick order dispatched the Russian with a true shot to the heart.

Another Russian burst in from the back room, his attack rifle on full automatic, his finger glued to the trigger. The air six feet above the floor buzzed like a hive of killer bees. Had he used more control and less courage, he would have wiped the Phoenix detachment from the slate of the living. Instead he let the muzzle climb and sprayed the ceiling.

Katz's shotgun chomped away at the man's flesh, and Katz looked away, reminded again that a shotgun was not a neat instrument.

"We no longer have a monopoly on guns," Manning commented.

"McCarter," Katz ordered, "get in the back room. Cover our rear and see if we can retreat that way."

McCarter nodded, then snatched an automatic weapon from the wall and, weapon blazing, entered the rear room. Katz took more loaded guns and slid them into the back room. From the exchange of bullets he could judge that there was no safe exit out the back.

Manning was also clearly engaged in battle. "Katz," he called. "We got trouble up front."

"Tell me when there are new developments."

"I'm serious."

Katz, behind the counter, stuffed a Ruger Super Blackhawk KS-411 into his waistband. With its ten and a half inch untapered barrel, it had the weight necessary to hold down the .44 Magnum shells.

Manning fired a short burst and told Katz the next development outside.

"They're in the tavern, trying to reach the roof." He shot again, and across the street somebody toppled as though it was suddenly all too much for him. "If they get there, they'll be shooting straight down our throats."

The Phoenix Force leader got the message. The tavern's brick front extended a foot or two above the roof behind it. A few of the weapons in the store could chop away the brick protective wall—if there was time, which there would not be.

If the armed force outside had grenades or tear gas the Phoenix trio's odds for survival were highly unfavorable.

Katz let his eyes sweep the room. Spotting what he wanted, he moved away from cover to reach a cabinet under the gun displays. Enemy bullets pocked the cabinets, then went wild as Manning returned fire.

"Here, use these." With that, Katz rolled a string of old-fashioned fragmentation grenades across the floor.

Manning pulled a pin and tried to find a position on the floor from which he could lob a grenade across the wide street. An overhand toss exploded in the far gutter. It may have made the enemy duck, but it left the tavern unscathed.

"I gotta stand up to make it," Manning said without confidence. He feared he could not stand long enough to throw.

"Suicide," Katz said.

"You got that right."

"Then get up and throw when I yell."

"Why?"

"Trust me."

Katz collected four grenades, palmed one, released the pin and threw it into the street. From his position he could get no more than halfway. But heads on both sides ducked as shrapnel screamed simultaneously into the tavern and the gun shop.

He followed it with another and another, then hesitated, giving the enemy a chance to raise their heads to see if more was to follow.

Katz flung the remaining grenade, and every head took cover, including that of Gary Manning.

"Go!" Katz yelled.

"What? Now?"

"Now."

With a sense of finality and feeling the danger every bit, Manning stood up, his body exposed from his waist to the top of his head. To the sharpshooters across the street, he was a perfect target.

He pulled the pin and let the handle fly. Ticking off a couple of beats, he fixed his eyes on the one Katz had thrown. It would go off in milliseconds, and he would still be standing.

Unlike the Russians across the street, he ignored the all-powerful urge to seek cover.

"Throw," Katz told him.

Manning was cutting the time too close.

The unexploded grenade Katz had thrown would keep the enemy down just long enough for them to figure they had been duped, ten to fifteen seconds at the most.

"Throw!" Katz yelled again.

Manning threw. The explosion caught three Russians who were poking their heads up to see why the other grenade had not popped.

They got no more chances in this life to be curious or anything else.

Now every head was down across the street, and Manning was throwing the powerful eggs one after another.

Katz fed him from a cache of M-59 fragmentation grenades.

It was like the Fourth of July in the tavern. Men leaped from the roof as the building collapsed with a creaking and crashing.

Taking advantage of the lull, Katz made a dash for the light switch, knowing that the darker it was, the better off they were.

Manning took a breather and thought that he needed a strategic overview of the situation.

"Okay, Katz, you're the brains. What have we stumbled into?"

"A school for spies, saboteurs and agitators. They must bring in agents who are already fluent in English and make them live here until they can fit smoothly into American society."

"Why did they call it Cheyenne?"

"Cheyenne used to have a lot of missiles and control elements nearby. Still does. With luck, graduates from here can work their way into the defense system."

"But where is the urgency?"

Katz shook his head. "I don't know why, but I trust that CIA kid. He apparently died to get his warning through. I think we're sitting on a nuke. Whatever it is, we'd better break it up."

"How?"

Katz shrugged. "As I see it, we've got to level the town and annihilate all the inhabitants."

"But that's impossible."

In the dark Yakov Katzenelenbogen sighed. "We can try. We have to try, anyway, because we don't have much choice."

6

In the Yalta hotel room, Rafael Encizo paced the floor the way he had in Fidel Castro's prison. In the dank Cuban cell, he had made three stretching strides forward, sharply about-faced, and retraced his steps hour upon determined hour of endurance-building exercise.

When he hadn't been walking, he did sit-ups or push-ups. At night he'd ground away at the wall beneath his bed with a wire coil from the springs. He'd timed and studied every routine of the vicious guards and the other prisoners.

Encizo had known through every waking minute of his long confinement at Principe prison that eventually he would escape. He would dig his way out. Or he would overpower a guard and dodge through automatic rifle fire spraying from the prison walls and guard towers. He was determined to succeed or die while trying.

To condition himself, he ran in place every other day until he dropped. He would be in perfect shape and with well-developed endurance when the chance came to escape.

And it did. Finally after surviving gunfire, starvation, and shark attack, he lurched onto American soil and sucked in freedom like a man cut free of the hangman's noose.

That was why Phoenix Force appealed to him. It was a "can do, will do" organization. While he could not fight Fidel Castro directly, he could strike at other dictators and cruel madmen with the same monstrous mindset.

Equally important, he rarely had to stay inactive or holed up in a room for any length of time.

Tonight he felt imprisoned again. The magnificently appointed suite was as good as a cell of steel and reinforced concrete.

Under orders to wait until Katz and the two others returned or were not back by the preset deadline, he paced and fidgeted impatiently.

"Madre de Dios," he muttered when he checked his waterproof, shockproof, non-light-emitting watch. "They should be back by now."

He held the electronic piece to his ear as if he could hear it ticking away the minutes.

He ran his hand nervously through his hair and tried to keep his deep brown eyes from darting nervously around the room.

Hal Brognola's edict that the team members would carry no weapons whatsoever added to the tension. Encizo felt naked. His clothes, though, were more chic than he normally wore because the commander at Stony Man Farm had bought everything for all five men. It was his way of emphasizing that he did not want any objects carried into Russia that could be converted to offensive or defensive use by his highly innovative troops.

"Relax," Calvin Thomas James said from the far bed where he lay with his fingers laced behind his head.

"They aren't even due back for another twenty minutes."

The handsome black with the pencil-thin mustache had forced himself to relax. He used biofeedback techniques he had learned while he was working for his black belt in tae kwon do.

"Remember what McCarter said about this mission," James suggested.

Encizo shoved his hands deep into his pockets and frowned. "Yeah. He called it a 'bloody cakewalk.' That's what an English mercenary said about the Bay of Pigs. With the United States back of us, training us in advanced guerrilla tactics at Fort Meade, and all, how could Castro hold out against counter-revolutionaries like us? And look how that turned out."

The ill-fated invasion of Cuba by refugees from Castro's Communist regime was never far from Encizo's thoughts. "*El Sargento.* That's what we called Batista, the 'little sergeant' who became a dictator. So I helped Castro overthrow him. Can you believe that? I really believed in Fidel. And what happens? He's a Communist. The only difference is a Communist dictator owns it all. You work for him or you don't eat."

"So you went back in the Bay of Pigs fiasco to throw Castro out. And spent a decade in prison when President Kennedy didn't come through with air cover."

"I'm going back someday. Someday I'll get another shot at Fidel. Meanwhile, I'm practicing on all the other scum in the world."

He stopped pacing.

The prison-induced claustrophobia struck again, here in a luxurious, spacious hotel suite. It occurred often when he was in a Communist country.

"We should go after Katz and the guys. Right now."

The lanky Calvin James left the bed and stood before the mirror above the sink. He studied his own high cheekbones and decided he needed a shave. He plugged in the adaptable electric razor. Its contented buzzing infuriated the Cuban.

"How can you shave now? Turn it off. We might not hear the telephone ring."

James smiled at his friend's irritation and finished as quickly as he could.

A knock at the door startled Encizo into action. "That'll be them," he said, approaching the door with a relieved look on his face.

Calvin James held up his hand in a warning. "Wait," he said, and his precaution pulled the Cuban up short.

Their team members would not knock on the door. From the start of the tour, those who had been assigned the actual surveillance job had kept their distance from the others. Brognola had been specific about that. Although the security-minded Russians would suspect five single male tourists regardless, the goal was to make every effort to keep the two detachments apart.

"They're just supposed to pass the door laughing and joking if the mission went well," James reminded his friend.

Encizo dampened his anticipation and took a glass of brandy on the rocks from the built-in bar and downed a hearty swig.

He did not drink to steady his nerves but wanted the alcohol on his breath when he answered the knock. Two men still in their room would look more ordinary if they appeared to be having a drink before a late dinner.

He wished, though, that he had a weapon. He had taken private lessons in karate and kung fu and was fully capable of killing with his bare hands, but he also knew that in certain cases a gun was usually decisive.

Calvin James picked up the ice bucket before he opened the door. The bucket was not much of a defensive weapon, but at least it was a solid and fairly hefty object. He called out jovially, "Yes, who is it?"

"Maria, your guide," said a familiar voice.

Encizo opened the door immediately. Deliberately he did not look beyond her to see if there was anyone else in the hall. Nor did they close the door behind her when she stepped into the room. Their objective was to avoid arousing the least suspicion.

"Come in, Maria. Have a drink. Tell us about tomorrow's itinerary," James told her.

"Nyet," she said, as though she wanted to make sure she lived up to a cartoonist's impression of a rule-bound Intourist guide. She wore a dark two-piece suit with pockets like those on a man's jacket. Her white blouse was so stiff and prim that the collar could have held her head in place.

From a shoulder strap hung the large purse in which she kept maps, a notebook listing the foreigners in her charge, and inner files that she guarded with the devotion due to the codes of the Russian Star Wars defense system.

Brusquely she brushed past both of them, opened the closet and stuck her head into the bathroom.

Encizo resorted to some quick thinking. "Oh, you came to see if we have fresh towels. How nice of you, Maria."

James said, "Everything is perfect. Almost up to American standards."

"A bar of soap would be nice, though," Encizo added.

She looked at them huffily. "That is not why I come." She stooped as if to look under the beds.

"Go ahead. Look. No women. None of them have given in to our charms yet."

Encizo laughed. "I didn't know you Russians were so...so..."

"Puritanical," James finished for him.

"Where are they?" she asked abruptly.

Encizo nodded. "Under the beds, of course."

She stooped, lifted the quilts and looked carefully under each bed.

"There is no one there. You lie."

"Wishful thinking on my part."

"What are you talking about?" she demanded. "I do not understand."

"Girls," James said. "We wished we had a girl under there."

"I have no time for nonsense. Where are the others?"

"What others?"

"The other three men travelling together. They are with you? No?"

"On the same tour, yeah."

"You know them from before."

"Not me." Encizo then looked inquiringly at his companion. "How about you, buddy?"

James shook his head with a disinterested look, but internally he tensed. Trouble was pressing in upon them, and he slowly inched his way between the guide and the door while he spoke to her in soothing tones. "Actually, we didn't know each other until we met on the tour. Guaranteed share, you know. Costs nearly twice as much if you want a single room."

He was behind her now and able to look both ways, up and down the corridor. There was no one except an old woman drowsing in a chair near the elevators. Many Russian hotels and public establishments still had the grandmotherly women who helped guests with fresh towels or assisted them with other minor attentions needed for their comfort. But mostly they were the last rung in the Communist hierarchy of KGB surveillance.

The guide whirled around when James closed the door as quietly as he could.

Her angry eyes and gestapo mouth betrayed her. She was not going to stop with a simple check of the room. She thought she was onto something suspicious.

She tried to step around Encizo to reach the telephone, but he moved to block her path. Then she spun around to face Calvin James. "Open the door. What are you doing?" She was not certain whether they were enemy agents or rapists.

"Now, what about the other three men?" James asked.

"They have disappeared."

"Disappeared?"

"They are not in their rooms."

"Maybe they went down to the bar."

"No. They appear to have left the hotel." Her gaze darted about as if she was seeking an escape route or a weapon with which to protect herself.

Encizo raised his hands. "So they went for a walk. That is not forbidden, is it?"

"Nothing is forbidden for regular tourists. This is a free country. But they are different, and you are different."

She sidled away, trying to reach the telephone between the beds.

Calvin James knew the situation was deteriorating rapidly. If she called in her superiors, he and Encizo might be detained. The same was true of the other three when they returned. While their cover had been well documented, an in-depth inquiry could possibly disclose their true identity.

He thought that maybe he could save the situation by using charm on her.

"Hey, lady," he called, advancing toward her with a smile, his right hand still holding the ice bucket. "I don't know those three guys from Adam." She scowled at him. "I guess you don't know who Adam is, seeing as how you folks are atheists and all, but what I mean..."

"I know Adam. We are not fools just because we do not believe in fairy tales."

"We'll find the others," Encizo volunteered. "You don't want to spoil their vacation."

"That's bad PR," James added.

"I must call my superiors."

They could no longer maneuver her away from the phone, so they advanced on her. "Let's talk this over."

She touched the phone, and Encizo put his hand over hers. "It's too late, guy."

She glanced from one to the other, and there was growing fear in her eyes.

Something about the woman reminded Calvin James of his sister. Maybe it was the sudden vulnerable expression on her face that brought back to memory the better times, before she died of a heroin overdose.

He knew he ought to neutralize the angry-eyed guide, but he perspired just thinking of her dying in his hands.

She spared him from further dilemma when she took the initiative.

She jabbed one hand down into the enormous handbag, and the Phoenix Force warriors grabbed for her. James caught her wrist while it was still inside the purse. Encizo got hold of her around the neck, choking off her scream with one hand and covering her mouth with the other.

Only when he felt the jab of pain in his thigh did Calvin James recognize that they had made a mistake.

Her right hand had come out of the purse empty, but the other hand had dug a knife from the mannish pocket of her jacket.

Instinct saved him.

He had pinned her down over the nightstand and crushed her with his bulk. She had no space in which to build up momentum for plunging the knife through his clothes and deep into the hard muscles of his leg. The wound was superficial.

Grunting in pain, he got hold of her wrist with a lightning-fast motion and twisted until the knife fell free. He retrieved it and placed the point to her throat.

"Don't," Encizo cautioned. "She will boil in her own juices when this gets heard higher up."

"So what do we do now? She'll turn us in to the police or the KGB."

The woman shook her head negatively to convince them that she would do nothing if they set her free.

"We tie her up and go to the American embassy."

"That's in Moscow. Maybe there's a consulate here."

"Good. You cut up the sheets. I'll hold our Maria."

James bathed the woman in a wide, cheery smile, and they set to work quickly, gagging and tying her to the commode in the bathroom.

Then James bandaged his leg, donned clean trousers, then pocketed her knife.

They had just left the room when they nearly collided with the old woman from the end of the hall. Her arms were loaded with fresh towels.

She added urgency to their problems. Unless they could divert her and thus prevent her from sounding an alarm, they were not going to get the hour or two of head start that they had expected.

Encizo tried what he could. "No, no, *señora*. No more towels."

She twisted around them, intent on entering the room. Calvin, however, put a friendly, though firm, arm across her shoulders and urged her to walk with them to the elevator.

We ought to get rid of her, he thought. We ought to get rid of both of the women.

But the mission had a low priority and didn't justify drastic measures at this point.

He could not harm the old woman. Instead he held her affectionately, talking reassuringly to her until the elevator doors opened. When Calvin and Encizo had entered and the doors began to close, he could see her rushing in the direction of their room.

"Damn," he said.

"So what do we do now?" Encizo asked.

As one of the youngest members of the team, James usually deferred to others when it came to important decisions. Now Encizo was asking him.

"We could head for the wharf. Try to get aboard a ship with a western registration."

"And what about Katz? Manning? McCarter? They're just about overdue."

"We can head north, but we could miss them if they're on their way here. Oh, hell, we can't do anything else. But we don't even know how they'll be coming back, whether by car or truck. They might have taken a bus."

"Doesn't matter," Encizo said. "We've got to try."

"Yeah. I know."

But as they stepped into the huge, echoing lobby, Calvin James had no confidence that they would leave Russia alive.

A mission that was supposed to be a cakewalk had just fallen into a deep, dark abyss. And there was no seeing to the bottom.

7

At the lobby desk, an assistant manager held a telephone to his ear. His face was a mask of dread. Horrified by what he was hearing, he curled his free hand into a nervous, shaking fist.

He raised his head, searching frantically for help.

For an instant the worried Calvin James thought the man was looking for him, and when the Russian made a motioning sign, the black American nearly pointed a finger at his own chest as if to say, "Who, me?"

Encizo stopped him from carrying out the gesture and said, "Keep walking. And smile."

"Yeah, but..."

Then James saw to whom the manager was beckoning. Two men in identical dark suits had been standing near one of the huge stainless-steel pillars that reached three stories to the mosaic ceiling of the lobby.

Security men, James guessed. Maybe KGB.

They had been lazily sweeping their gaze across the milling crowd of foreigners. Their boredom showed, but when they saw the man at the desk summon them, they restricted themselves to a brisk but circumspect walk.

The security men reached the counter just as the two Phoenix Force men, easily agitated because they were rushing without trying to show it, pushed open the glass exterior doors.

A doorman in full uniform was leaning against the wall, yawning. Officially tips were verboten in Russia. Although few workers were ever fired, without incentives, service personnel worked in a slow-motion daze.

"Can you get us a cab?" Encizo asked, hiding his anxiety while inwardly fuming at the doorman's indifference.

The Russian pointed with a limp thumb at the lead taxi that headed up a row of four.

"Hey, taxi!" James called. He was accustomed to the legendary drivers of New York, but he could see this one laugh at the summons, put his head back on the headrest and close his eyes.

Without a word the two Americans split and approached the cab from either side.

Encizo opened the front passenger door, slid in and reached across to turn on the engine. The Russian said something vulgar and grabbed for the key.

He didn't manage to accomplish his objective as Calvin James opened the driver's door thrust in both hands and caught the cabbie by his belt and his neck. Before the Russian could understand what was happening he was ejected from the vehicle. He fell on his back and had not regained his footing when James took his place behind the wheel and jerked the car into gear, leaping ahead.

Every Russian in the area came alive.

The doorman courageously scrambled to impose himself in front of the fleeing vehicle, but luckily for him the front of the car had passed before he could do that. Instead of being crushed, the straight fender sent him spinning like a top.

Behind the Americans the lined-up cabs lurched forward in pursuit.

By then the two security guards from inside dashed out to the curb, pistols in hand. They fired wildly up the hotel driveway, and tourists and residents scurried for cover.

Encizo cursed, "Aw, hell. I should have known Brognola would never send us on a real vacation."

"And now how do we get out of this mess?" his partner asked of no one in particular.

At the end of the hotel drive, the taxi swerved into an obstacle course of Russian vacationers strolling in the streets as well as filling both sidewalks.

James held his hand to the horn.

People scattered like a flock of birds at the sound of a shotgun.

As the Phoenix duo sped on, cars slid to a stop, took unexpected turns into alleys, and jumped the curbs and stopped, their front ends showered with glass from blasted storefronts.

"Now we're in the muck," James said. "We should have let the guide call her superiors."

"Should-haves will buy you zilch," Encizo said, bracing himself in the churning vehicle. A parade of angry pursuers jockeyed for position behind the escaping car. Over his shoulder Encizo saw the other taxi drivers heading up the chase. No doubt the KGB pair were bringing up the tail.

Six blocks from the hotel a siren wailed. Amber lights flashed threateningly from a cross street and from straight ahead. Like a kamikaze pilot, one driver roared toward the Phoenix Force car. Taking the center of the street, he was intent on a head-on collision.

"Watch him!" the Cuban warned.

"Hold on, we're taking a hard right."

"No!" the Cuban said persuasively, knowing what lay ahead.

Their taxi went into a tire-screaming skid and spun into the turn precariously relying on two wheels.

The side street they had entered was not a wide boulevard, and the stands of an outdoor vegetable market overflowed the curbs. The space left open for traffic was barely enough for a carefully driven car. For an instant James was tempted to play out a hackney scene from a hundred old movies. The flying vegetables and the ones squashing against the car might make a funny epitaph for his brief career. And at the moment he expected that at the best the odds were in favor of a short retirement as the guest of their Russian hosts.

"Don't do it," Encizo advised.

"Okay, but there are no guarantees."

One stand lost a leg and sent a train of squash into the street. At another outdoor shop, the awning fell like a funeral shroud over the head of the irate vendor.

If he had dared, the American would have slowed to see how his pursuers managed the route through the market. Instead he saw a chance to gain a few more yards, and swung to the right to straddle the sidewalk. He was determined to lengthen or at least maintain his and Encizo's life expectancies, which right now he estimated at ten minutes.

By the time they had cleared the shopping district and entered a neighborhood of four- to six-story apartments, drab in design and poorly constructed, the trailing caravan had added at least two more police vehicles. Some of the taxis had dropped from the race and left it to the professionals.

"Health spas," Encizo observed, trying to lessen the tension. He pointed at the surroundings like a guide. "Factories all over the Soviet Union own baths here for their workers. If you fill the quota, talk the Party line, and maybe pay a little under the table— Calvin!"

James saw the narrowing road and swerved off the pavement, barely missing a pair of sturdy trees. Then bullets punched through the rear window, showering them with slivered glass.

"Oh, great," James said flatly. They were out of the city now, and projectiles continued to thump the body of the taxi and chip the pavement as the pursuers tried for the tires.

Encizo was remarkably calm and optimistic. "We're going to rescue the other three guys," Encizo said calmly. "This road should take us close enough that we won't have more than a ten-minute run through the woods."

He took a map from the glove compartment and unfolded it as the taxi took desperate twists and curves in an effort to avoid bullets that finally hit the windshield and turned it into a spiderweb of cracks.

"There's a town ahead," Encizo said, tapping a point on the map.

James worked the wheel with furious and creative determination. The taxi sliced into one ditch, then climbed out and dipped into the other. He tapped his brakes to flash the taillights and force his pursuers to pump their own brakes. They learned quickly not to trust his signals.

"How far is the town?" James shouted.

"We're coming up on it now."

"The guys behind us have had time to radio ahead."

"Yeah, there will be a block this side of town. They won't want us to get a lot of streets to choose from."

"Damn," James said as he peered at headlights ahead. They appeared to be at right angles to the road.

"They're using a car for the block, just like I figured," Encizo intoned over the noise. "That's just what we wanted."

"Yeah," James said cynically. "Everything is coming up roses."

"Jam the brakes. Give me a little left turn and then a right so the guys ahead won't see me doing my graceful swan dive."

James nodded acknowledgment.

"Go, Encizo, go."

"I'm gone, man."

Ahead of them a police car fully blocked the road.

Encizo unlatched the passenger door and waited for the momentum of the sudden braking action to fling it open. Then he leaped for the side of the road. He rolled, bounced and skidded before plunging into a foot of drainage water.

He held his breath and kept his face down in the muck as if he were dead or unconscious.

Still in the taxi, James saw two police officers waiting at the roadblock. They carried automatic rifles, ready for the kill, but their number was manageable.

No problem, the young black reassured himself. Once he managed to get out of the taxi alive, he would be able to neutralize two country cops with his bare hands.

He gave himself two seconds to refresh his memory on the trick McCarter had taught him.

"Now," he shouted aloud.

He snugged his seat belt, unlatched the door on his side, turned sharply and stomped on the brakes.

The car went into a skid, the tires screaming.

He released the steering wheel and prepared to unfasten his seat belt as the car assumed control. It did as it damn pleased, sliding crosswise on the road. The left wheels left the pavement. The taxi persisted on its chosen direction and the only way was to roll.

Momentum obliged.

The car slid on its right side for a few yards, then the next thing James knew he was upside down. Dirt from the floor and papers from the glove compartment rained on him. The roof was collapsing, squeezing down against his head, forcing his face into the steering wheel.

There was pain. All over. Not in vital organs, he hoped.

When the battered chassis stopped, he unlatched his belt but found that he couldn't move.

Outside one of the police cars from Yalta made a panic stop. The second smashed into the rear of the lead vehicle, setting off a deafening chain reaction.

From ahead, the two local police officers instinctively leaped to the shoulder of the road. One landed safely and rolled until he regained his upright stance. He made straight toward the driver's side of the overturned taxi.

The door was open, but a stunned Calvin James was having difficulty extricating himself from the compressed interior.

Holding his weapon in one hand, the officer helped the black foreigner. The taxi reeked of gasoline, and both of them were anxious to be a safe distance away when the inevitable explosion of the fuel tank occurred.

"Thanks," James said once he was in the open air. Then he kicked the cop in the groin, yanked the AK-47 from him and cracked him on the head with the butt. "Sorry," James added.

In the other gutter the second officer was searching for the body he thought he had seen thrown from the cab.

Encizo, dripping with muck, his face turned to one side to breathe, stabbed out his left hand to catch the man by the ankle.

In one swift movement Encizo pulled the officer off balance and into the drainage ditch. He stunned him with a kick to the face and then forced the Russian's head into the water, struggling to hold it there. Then he picked up the attack rifle and took several spare clips from the nearly drowned man.

He swung around in time to see the other policeman trying to recover from his pain to tackle James. No more than five square inches of the Russian officer's head was exposed. James was unwillingly providing body armor for the rest and trying to break a choke hold that threatened to gag him into unconsciousness.

The Cuban took one quick look at their pursuers. One of their cars was stuck nose-down in the ditch, and a second car rested on its top, its wheels spinning.

A would-be hero raced an official car up the shoulder, two wheels on the edge of the pavement and the other two spurting a rooster tail of water from the flooded ditch. He provided a fine target and offered Encizo a good starting point for his offensive.

The Cuban-born warrior rattled off a steady string of bullets. They eliminated the windshield, found the driver and added more wreckage to the growing roadblock.

A half dozen of the Russian officers on foot had unintentionally formed a straight line across the road. They stormed the overturned taxi, the lights from their own stalled vehicles silhouetting them, making them perfect targets.

Encizo squeezed off six steady shots.

The pursuers went down in a neat row, either as casualties or as the result of quick thinking. The Phoenix Force expert put bullets in the last three men just to be certain they were out of the blood sport before he turned toward his friend.

What he saw made him very fast in feeding in a new clip of ammo.

James was choking to death. To aim carefully Encizo had the time it takes a clock to tick. Russian reinforcements were on the way.

"Sorry, Calvin," he called. "If I miss, you're better off dead anyway."

He fired.

The bullet tore a path in the side of the man's skull, and blood squirted freely and with great force.

The cop lost the choke hold and flew backward, freeing James. "Nice shooting," he said with a weak grin.

"We aren't out of this yet. Get to the car ahead and be ready for a fast break. I'll provide cover."

The last part of his sentence was lost in a burst of gunfire as he opened up on the enemy reinforcements.

He hit one in the knee. That one did a somersault. He grazed another, and a third one, hit in the shoulder, was wrenched backward. The others fled for cover.

While Encizo kept the enemy down as he backed away, James slid into the driver's seat of the police car.

"Let's get out of here," he called.

The police car that had served as the original roadblock was pointed away from the vehicular carnage. It was moving before the Cuban fired the rest of his bullets and jumped into the passenger seat.

Seconds later the speedometer hit its peak.

It was a mile before Calvin James breathed easily enough to pose a question. "Now what?"

"Wasn't that enough?"

"We need a plan."

"We go rescue the other guys like we intended to do all along."

"You think they need rescuing more than us?"

"How's that?"

"We're in a stolen police car. We left a dozen security men and cops dead or moaning. There isn't a cold enough place in all Siberia for them to send us."

"Relax, *amigo*. Those guys still breathing are stuck behind a junkyard."

"They have mobile radios. They'll call ahead. We'll be recognized immediately in this thing."

Encizo leaned his head back. "Turn on the siren and the flashing lights."

"We'll be even more visible."

Encizo tapped his friend. "Think. The first car we catch up with is going to pull off the road. We swap vehicles. *Comprende?*"

James closed his eyes for a moment. He appeared calm, but he would not have sold himself an insurance policy for longer than the next five minutes.

8

The "Reverend" Arnold Vulcan was in a towering rage. He was poised on the steps of his church, his face flushed, his eyes burning in their sockets. Clenching and unclenching his fists, he fought for control. Had he a saber or scimitar, he might have come down from his perch to slash and cut anything or anyone who dared cross his path.

One of his frequent fantasies flashed into his mind, and he saw himself on horseback, riding hard and cutting a killing path through his enemies without remorse.

In his late teens he had served as a guard in Siberian labor camps. There he learned the enormous power of cruelty. Kindly guards were rewarded with friendship by their charges. Cruelty made him superior to the gaunt, broken individuals who worked under him. They hated him, but they worked. Mistreatment made them surpass his production quota, an achievement that caught his superior's attention.

The other wardens feared him, too, feared he might rise above them and treat them as he treated the prisoners. They praised him and assumed he was a protégé of the higher-ups. Because they feared him, they helped him grow in stature.

Ever since his education in the camps, he had blended cruelty with fear and, more recently, had learned how to handle his superiors.

More than life itself, the rulers feared losing their sometimes slowly acquired amenities. Losing their special status that made them different from the classless Communist society was their greatest fear.

Vulcan was a bestial man. He would allow no one to unseat those above him even if it required killing interlopers or torturing those who threatened the stature of those currently in control.

The implied promise remained unspoken and when he was ready, his superiors moved him another notch higher. And each of the aging rulers thought Vulcan was his own special protégé and protector. Meanwhile he shared one success after another with the aspirants in the Politburo.

His brainchild—Cheyenne, Wyoming—blended those factors. The inhabitants were as good as prisoners who would unwittingly support his rise to power.

The project would propel him to share in the authority invested in those sheltered by the Kremlin walls. It already kept him in the eyes of the Party hierarchy.

The new Cheyenne project would take him farther yet. But some maniac was trying to destroy it. He let his eyes take in the scene again, and he could not believe what he saw.

Bodies littered the main street of his fiefdom. The dead lay in positions of defeat where they fell. Several were face down on the pavement, soaking in their own blood. A man sat against the door of ComputerLand. His arms were limp at his sides, as though he had suffered from the summer heat and slumped with exhaustion. His tongue lolled like a panting dog's.

Vulcan knew the man well. He had been crucial in planning the upcoming mission.

"Who did this?" Vulcan roared. "Who dared do this to me?"

He came down one step.

He imagined any number of enemies who might attempt to destroy his creation. They were all inside the government. Small, incompetent challengers knew they had to destroy Vulcan if they were to achieve their own fantasies.

"Are these traitors from our own ranks?" It was easy to believe that some of his subjects were in the employ of his enemies. Traitors were all around him.

He would see them executed after he tortured them in the KGB ways. No perpetrator of such a crime against him deserved to die easily.

The next minute his eyes recorded a ghastly sight that fed the raging fire inside of him.

Four corpses formed a semicircle in front of the gun shop. One man had reached as far as the sidewalk.

No one had ventured out to police the dead. Several broken and bloodied forms showed signs of life. The hands of one man clawed the pavement, reaching for the gun he had been firing. Another dying man sat in the gutter, holding an H&K MP-5 in both of his shaking hands. The German chatter gun pumped slugs into the gaping window of the gun shop.

When his weapon's hammer clicked on empty, a short familiar burst of an AK-47 from inside made his body dance.

Others appeared to be breathing.

"You out there," Katz called from inside. "Do you want a truce long enough to gather your wounded?"

Vulcan came down another step.

"Who is that? Is it one of ours?" He shoved his hand inside his black suitcoat and withdrew a Beretta 92-F. He treasured the 9 mm semiauto because it was the U.S. Military replacement for the aged Colt .45 government model.

It was tough like him. Rugged like him. "Truce, hell." He laughed loud enough to be heard in the shop.

He fingered the trigger in a single-hand hold. The first shot was double-action, but each of the others took only a light touch of the forefinger. He fired all sixteen shells randomly through the empty window frame. From his position nearly parallel to the storefront, he knew his shots were useless unless a lucky ricochet caught one of the devils who had gone mad in his favorite store.

Vulcan did not care.

He released the empty clip and replaced it with a full one from the breast pocket on the other side of his jacket. His finger felt good on the trigger. Mentally he was lost in a muddle of troubling questions. He was infected, too, by the fierce temper that had plagued him since childhood.

He took the last step and started toward the store, and he might have walked straight into combat if his chief aide had not stopped him.

"Reverend Vulcan, don't," Colin Edge said. He was American by birth and had lived in New York City where his parents served the Russian ambassador to the United Nations. He hated the land of his birth with a special passion that he never let anyone else understand. Secretly, his hate was caused by the fact that he damned every American for letting his parents drag him bodily to an Aeroflot jetliner when he had been fourteen and force him into the poverty of mind and goods that he found the USSR to be. "Stop or you'll be killed."

Vulcan laughed. "Killed? By whom?"

He could not conceive that anyone was capable of hurting him as long as he held a functioning gun in his hands. With the Beretta at intermediate ranges, he had outscored men with hunting rifles.

"Colin is right," the woman who called herself Ann Cardwell said. "You would kill one, probably two, maybe wound a third, but there may be more inside. Besides, nothing is worth risking your life for at this point in our mission."

Colin Edge moved his hands slightly, motioning with his fingers to warn her not to tell Vulcan that there was something he couldn't do.

Although Edge was taller than his superior, he appeared to be a small man. His shoulders were hunched defensively as a lasting result of the beatings and mind-altering drugs administered in the mental hospital where he had spent years for his outspoken defiance of authority. He held his arms pressed close to his side as though he were a man in a crowded elevator. His milky gray eyes had a slightly vacant look at times, and he unconsciously made scrubbing motions with his hands whenever he was disturbed.

Gray hair and a gaunt face made him look older than his forty years. He appeared to be totally devoted to Vulcan, although actually his only concern was the security he felt he gained by his unswerving loyalty.

To him, Vulcan reigned as a high priest with protective powers when he cared to dispense them. So, Edge obeyed and followed except now when the danger was real. Then he protected his lifeline.

Vulcan took another step, as though he wouldn't be detained.

"Go ahead. Be a fool," Ann Cardwell told him. "I will take your place."

The words were exactly right. He stopped. No one would lead the mission except him. "Who are they?" he demanded, breathing like the bull tormented by a matador. "Who allowed that to happen? And that?" He pointed at the heap of smoking ruins that the tavern had become, then at the gun shop.

Neither Ann Cardwell nor Edge answered.

Ann felt no guilt although she knew Vulcan would eventually give his superiors a sacrificial lamb. She had been the first to come running to him with news that there were strangers in the McDonald's store, but he had not taken the matter very seriously.

Although entrance and exit from his Cheyenne were officially restricted, they were never bothered by strangers. The security men who were supposed to patrol the perimeter were not professional. They were cadre who wanted only to be shipped to the United States as quickly as possible, and they had never met any threat.

As Vulcan looked around yet again, the enormity of the slaughter nearly overpowered him. His knees became water. He had no idea what could have interfered with his project in such a drastic manner, and his voice threatened to betray his fear and his clouded mind.

He became terrified although he did all he could to hide his fear. Standing on the church steps, somewhat exposed, helped conceal that fear.

"Shall I call in the police from Yalta?" Ann Cardwell asked.

"Police?" he tried to sound incredulous.

Colin Edge suggested, "The army, then?"

Vulcan imagined the complications if he admitted he could not protect his own creation.

"What army?" He laughed.

"Why, the Russian army, sir."

"To stop three men?"

"Three men in a gun shop with a wide selection of weapons and thousands of rounds of ammunition. Grenades. Smoke bombs," Ann said in support of Colin's suggestion.

Vulcan pretended that he considered the idea ridiculous. "They might be our own people."

"They are not," she said.

"You do not know everyone here."

"I know these are not our people. One had an artificial hand. No one with such a flaw would be allowed here."

"That does not mean we need outsiders. We have an entire town composed of young- to middle-aged men and women. All are trained in weapons. All of them have one or more guns in their house that they target-practice with five days a week."

"But the intruders have all the guns and ammunition they need inside the gun shop. The army would have flame throwers, tear gas, things like that. We would lose no more of our own people."

Forget our own people, he wanted to tell her. He could cover the loss with paperwork. Those in the Kremlin accepted human losses unless they became common knowledge.

"No army. No police. We have a twenty-man security force."

"Five of them were found dead in the forest," Colin Edge said softly. "More are still searching the woods."

"Searching the woods when the obvious assassins are here in the center of our city? Call them back immediately."

"Yes, Reverend Vulcan."

"At least half a dozen of our people have been killed in the street already," Ann Cardwell reminded the leader. "More are seriously wounded."

"Are any of those assigned to our next mission wounded or dead?" he asked coldly.

"No," Colin Edge responded. "I sheltered them immediately."

"Good."

"It would be better not to lose any of our own people. We should call for outside help." Ann Cardwell was the one person who did not cower before Vulcan.

"No. No. No. How often must I explain? This is a highly sensitive project. A stranger entering our area by mistake can be eliminated or otherwise distracted from recognizing what we do here. But we cannot bury soldiers or police forces without attracting attention."

"You are afraid," she said with amusement, "that your superiors will learn of this incursion."

Afraid you will report me too soon, Vulcan told himself.

"I will let them hear after we have left on our next mission. There are a few in high places who might panic when they hear about this incident and try to delay us. And an opportunity like the one we have now will never occur again." He paused to think before he continued. "No one in the Politburo would want me to allow three hooligans to interfere with my work, if they knew what an opportunity it is."

"Are they hooligans or a CIA suicide team?"

"What will it matter? They will be dead or in our custody soon."

Vulcan was in control of himself again. Cool, confident, a man of authority, he surveyed the situation. Only a handful of his men were still firing into the miniature fort held by the mysterious strangers. And those few were hiding behind buildings and other protective cover.

"Where is everyone else? Are the cowards in hiding?"

Colin Edge said, "They await your orders."

"Get fifty well-armed men. Cover front and back."

"Yes, sir."

Edge raised his hand as if to salute, catching himself just in time. Vulcan often went into rages when someone forgot details such as American civilians not saluting their superiors.

When he was gone, Ann said thoughtfully, "Fifty men against three, and one of them a cripple."

"Cripple?"

"I told you that one of them has lost an arm. He wears a device in its place."

When she had first mentioned that, the possible significance had not stirred Vulcan's thinking. "If you shared my lines to top espionage computer data, you would know there is a five-man American team, led by a one-armed man, that has been known to strike key targets and escape from incredible circumstances."

"There are only three. I am certain of that."

"Hmm. Possibly two more are about somewhere. If these are the men I think they are, we may suffer greater losses than I expected. Go find Colin. Have him put a hundred men into the assault. And arm yourself," he told her before stepping back into the church.

Alone, he pondered. Were the men cornered in the gun shop part of the five-man team? They had a name although his superiors had never told him. The assault force was an embarrassment to government security forces everywhere. No one wanted to admit it existed.

They were a myth, he had been told once.

He smiled.

What if he could wipe out three, perhaps all five, of the legendary group? Or capture one?

Yes, he hoped these were the men. He might knock off years in his drive to reach membership in the Politburo.

His ego soared to new heights.

And...ah...he would order his people to take one of the enemy alive. He would take the survivor to his superiors and insist upon being present during the interrogation. What a chance, he thought, highly stimulated by the possibilities. He felt young again.

9

"Katz, we got trouble back here," David McCarter said, leaving his post by the rear door of the gun shop long enough to gain his field leader's attention.

After nearly a half hour of firing powerful handguns indoors before they had time to put on ear protectors, none of the three was hearing well. Having heard the call, though, Katz moved into the rear room. He was careful to remain in the shadows, but even then a heavy-caliber bullet hissed past his head and whacked into the wallboard.

"Sharpshooter," he told the Englishman. "Is he giving you trouble?"

McCarter, using heavy packing crates for fortification, shook his head.

"He's in the tree near the fence. I'm going to get him the next time I see another target in that direction. No sense exposing myself twice when I can kill two bird brains with one volley. It's out there I'm worried about."

He pointed at the ranch-style homes backed against the alley that separated the business district from residential. Alleys also separated houses in the other blocks of homes.

At first Katz did not understand what McCarter was talking about.

He could have asked, but McCarter was a little crazy. He obviously wanted Katz to see for himself.

He saw the problem, although the only giveaway was an occasional flash of color, illuminated by streetlights two full blocks away. Dozens, maybe a hundred men, Katz estimated, were darting across the open spaces between the houses.

"They're bringing in more men for the finish," Katz remarked.

"I can get a few of them even at this range," McCarter said. "They're counting three before they send each man across that gap between the houses. I could get maybe four or five before they realize I can count, too."

"That's like putting your finger in the ocean instead of the dike," Katz observed. "But do it, anyway. If I don't figure a way out of this trap soon, we might as well take as many of them with us as possible."

McCarter carefully rose above his barricade and triggered the FAL that he was using at the moment. He fired before he saw one of the enemy actually break from behind the one house and attempt to dash to the next wall of cover. He was dead before he even thought he was exposed.

"See," McCarter crowed. "I'll let a couple more cross to be sure they're in the same cadence again before I wipe another one."

Katz sighed. "It doesn't matter much, does it?"

"What?"

McCarter was genuinely surprised. He was thinking only of body count. It kept his mind off the real problem.

"If you kill a third of them," Katz explained, "there'll still be seventy of them pouring lead through that door."

Already the door was nonfunctional. It hung open from one hinge. There was no closing it even if either side had wanted to.

"And if you stack up the other bodies like a cord of wood, they'd just bring in replacements."

McCarter's mind flicked to another worry. "If they throw a grenade in here, I'll just toss it back."

"They don't have grenades." Katz was thinking aloud. Against targets trapped inside a building, the weapon of choice would have been rifle grenades or a recoilless weapon with lots of bang. Or tear gas.

Or...he began to think of other possibilities. He raised one of the rifles McCarter had lined up neatly behind his barricade. McCarter, a sort of social misfit, had dedicated his life to learning every firearm as well as other lethal weapons. No doubt he was looking forward to testing each of the guns in living color. Besides, he did not have to reload when the Russians charged.

Katz picked up the Night-Eye binoculars lying near the weapons. He watched the place between the two houses and saw that the enemy consisted of civilians.

"We have to break out of this place. You just hold this end of the fort," Katz said. "I've got an idea."

He waited, then darted across an open space to the front, while McCarter calmly took aim and took out the sniper in the tree.

Halfway to the front room, Katz heard his name called again, this time by Gary Manning. He echoed David McCarter.

"We got big trouble here, Katz. Real big trouble."

He pointed to the right of the demolished tavern. The lights were off in the jewelry store, but there was enough illumination to see movement inside.

"And over there and there, too."

The story was the same in the dress shops and the adjoining shoe store.

Even as they watched, a number of men, in different configurations, tried to get closer.

Gary Manning aimed the M-16 A-1 rifle he had selected when he last ran out of ammunition for another weapon. With the Rock Island arsenal model, he led the enemy and began firing.

Manning looked pleased with himself, but Katz was indifferent and summed up the situation. "It doesn't matter. If they want to take the time, all they have to do is send a squad far enough up the street and then come straight through the lot to our wall."

"Meaning?"

"We can't stay here."

Manning was puzzled. "You mean we leave our own ammunition supply?"

"They'll get us eventually if we stay, no matter how many of them we kill first."

"Get us eventually? I thought that was a 'given.' There's no way we can get out of this alive."

Katz was emphatic. "We've stumbled onto a major KGB installation, a way of pouring exquisitely trained agents into the West. We have to get out of this alive. They are not calling in outside help, to maintain secrecy, and that gives us a slight chance. Not much, but it's better than nothing. And we have always achieved a 'must.'"

Manning looked skeptical. "Unfortunately we are about to break the string. We aren't getting out of this alive unless we surrender and, frankly, that's one thing I refuse to do."

Before he finished speaking, jacketed wad cutters began tearing up the rifles and shotguns that remained on the wall racks.

"Keep shooting," he told Manning. "Go wild whether you hit anybody or not. I need cover."

"My pleasure."

As the front of the gun shop became a steady stream of yard-long spears of fire from Manning's cache of weapons, Katz picked up another M-16 with a 40-round magazine and began stuffing his belt with assorted handguns and collected a cache of fully automatic rifles.

When he needed to move without crawling, he directed McCarter to put up a main line of resistance to match the frantic barrage Gary was spewing from the front of the store.

"You're on," McCarter called cheerfully from the rear. "Nobody's going to move out back until I'm out of ammo."

With more freedom of movement, Katz piled heavy wooden crates to form a U-shaped bunker along the wall shared with the supermarket.

He quickly pulled two grenade pins, dropped the hand-held bombs into the hole formed by the boxes, then leaped behind a sturdy counter. Manning ducked, too.

Despite the shooter's earmuffs they all wore, the twin explosions hammered them with a percussion effect, and the air filled with flying debris. A blinding cloud of dust billowed from the rubble. Briefly the battle fell into a lull as the men outside waited to see if some catastrophic explosion had done their job for them.

When he saw the hole in the wall and the grocery shelves beyond, Katz grabbed his stash of hoarded weapons and tossed them through the hole.

The attackers decided to become bolder, perhaps because they had taken the explosion as an encouraging sign. A few even came into the open. Some of them moved from cover, but neither Manning nor McCarter opened fire again until they had at least ten of the enemy in sight.

When the timing was right, they decked more than a dozen attackers and made the remainder more cautious. The Russians would take time to regroup, which gave a brief spell of time in which to make a move.

"Manning, McCarter, this way," Katz said as he climbed through the hole into the supermarket.

His plan was practically the equivalent of Russian roulette. He hoped to set the gun shop on fire and concentrate the opposition's attention on that while he and his partners broke out of the supermarket.

He had no plan for what they would do after they were in the open, but he knew his objectives: get one of them free and on the way to a Russian border. That person would alert Hal Brognola of the existence of Cheyenne, USSR. The two who remained behind would destroy as much of the town as possible.

Complications erupted the moment all three of them were inside the supermarket. Without warning, the west wall of the gun shop burst like a huge shell. Chunks of brick shrapnel stung the Phoenix Force detachment, and jagged slivers of studs and wallboard punctured their flesh.

When the wreckage settled, Katz could see the hood of a car, opened like a gaping jaw reacting to surprise. Obviously the car had been rammed against the wall.

A stunned driver crawled out of the wreckage, and Katz finished him with a short burst. The other Russians who were trying to get through the hole were an easy mark for Katz. As he trained his weapon on them he told Manning to get an armload of matches.

While Manning searched the aisles, gunfire from the gun shop was turning the supermarket into a shambles with dustings of flour and sugar and the rainlike effect of bottles cracking open.

Manning made his way back and dumped the matches around Katz.

"Head for the far front window," Katz directed. "Go through it the moment the fireworks begin back here."

Left alone, Katz fired a few more times, but he couldn't hope to hold off the enemy much longer.

"That's it, friends," Katz said to the invaders. "Come for the honey."

He lit one match and dropped it in the box he held in his hand. When the box ignited, Katz tossed it through the hole in the wall and toward the gunpowder display. He kept throwing the flaming matchboxes until his sense of timing told him to run.

He was at the front of the store when the gun shop went up. It blew in five directions, every way except down.

The common wall between the supermarket and the gun shop bulged, then collapsed, bringing down with it a quarter of the roof that battered Katz and nearly pinned him beneath its wreckage.

The front and rear of the gun shop sent out huge shafts of flame that consumed any Russian within range.

Blinded, choked by the powdered plaster, Katz scrambled straight through the hole in the front glass. The opening was there, just as he had expected.

Suddenly he was outside and found himself sprinting just behind Manning and McCarter.

They headed for the residential section before even one of the Russians spotted them.

As he rounded the first house and had cover to his back, Katz slowed. We've made it this far, he thought, then had to share his exultation with the others. "Gary, David, we did it. We're outside."

The pair stopped ahead of him, gasping for breath. They dropped their guns and bent over with their hands on their knees. The run from the supermarket had not winded them. It was the tension of the fight.

"And only eight or nine thousand miles from home," McCarter estimated.

Katz felt his enthusiasm waning as he sobered from the effects of the small victory. Obviously the other guys thought the mission was complete. There was another step to take, and he had to set the example. "You two take off. Contact Brognola as soon as you can. I'll stay around here awhile and do a little tidying up."

"You mean burning the town?" McCarter said.

"As much as I can. The place must be ultrasecret for the people here to avoid calling for outside help. So that provides me with an opportunity. I need an extra day or so around here. You two get out of Russia and get home to Stony Man."

Manning got a look on his face that was well-known by Phoenix Force members. He didn't often get to be like that, but when he did it meant that he would dig in his heels and wouldn't budge.

"Nobody is going to leave you here alone," he said.

"Calvin James and Encizo will probably be coming this way," Katz said. "Somebody has to stay here and tell them what happened. They'll give me a hand with the mop-up operation."

McCarter dropped to a sitting position.

In the background the gun shop was still putting on a brilliant display of pyrotechnics. The supermarket was consumed in flames that reached two or three stories in height. Across the street, the jewelry store was burning.

The church was the only building along that section of the street that was not involved.

"We'll tidy up now," McCarter said. "Then we'll all get out of here together."

"Well, I tried," Katz said with a shrug. "If you two insist on being underfoot..." He brightened up optimistically. "It doesn't look all that good, but I've been in as tough spots before, along with you, and managed somehow. There is a way. I'm sure!"

10

Vulcan stuck his head out from between the pews, a position he had taken when the exploding gun shop slammed bricks and hunks of debris against the church. Bullets, ignited by the ensuing fire, whomped steel jackets against the siding, but only the largest caliber slugs penetrated the walls.

As the ferocity of the conflagration subsided, he ventured up the aisle and cautiously opened the front door two full inches.

He called for both Ann Cardwell and his principal aide, Colin Edge.

Only Ann appeared, and there was the suggestion of a smirk on her sensuous-looking lips. He felt irritated, and at that moment he hated her. She had been in the streets, shouldering a gun, yet she appeared as cool and carefully groomed as ever.

He was reminded again how much he wanted her in his power, to do with as he wished. Such magnificently horrible things he would do to her, he thought gleefully.

However, his more immediate concern was that she would inform his superiors of the unexpected invasion before he had time to concoct a plausible and acceptable cover story.

That part of Vulcan's strategy involved Colin Edge, who was cutting off all communications to the outside world. He was due to be back at any moment to report on how successfully he'd carried out his task.

During the fighting Vulcan had attempted to draw Ann into the safety of the church, but she insisted upon remaining outside where she directed the fighting. She responded to his order and entered the church only after she had seen the town's fire brigade in action.

"Are the invaders dead?" he asked hopefully. "Did they go up in their own explosion?"

"No. Not all of them, at least."

"Not all?" He was losing his control. "How could anybody survive inside there?"

"They blew up the gun shop as a diversion," she said. "While our people had their heads down, I saw three men escape from the supermarket."

He was getting livid again. "The CIA invaders risk being killed by the explosions while our people cover their heads like the very picture of cowardice," he fumed. "I wish we had such heroic men on our side."

"The invaders, as you call them, had no choice. They could either take the risk of running, or be wiped out for sure."

"They were still more heroic. But what is the situation now?"

She pushed past him and went inside the church.

"What are you doing?"

She had gone to the altar and opened an electrical control panel behind the drapes. "Summoning the unit commanders," she said.

She pulled down one of several small levers in the control panel. The church bells pealed urgently.

Everyone in the town would recognize the coded signal.

"I'm ordering the unit commanders to have the townspeople change tactics completely. I have already spoken to several of the leaders."

"You're *ordering*?" Nothing infuriated him so much as anyone usurping his authority.

"I had no idea that you were still here when I had made the plan," she said. "When I was unable to find you during the action, I assumed you were dead or incapacitated."

He was stung that she had taken over his duties when in his impotent rage he had collapsed into helplessness and allowed himself to be convinced that he should take cover. Now he looked like a coward, while she acted like a brave leader. She must encounter some life-threatening difficulty on the next mission, he told himself, or she was capable of harming his reputation with his superiors. But before that came about, he had some other plans for her...

"All the women on the south side are to leave their homes," she continued. "They will move north of Main Street and protect themselves. Meanwhile—"

"Wait. You have not endangered any of those assigned to our next mission?"

"No. You are in no danger."

"What are you saying, that I am a coward?"

"No. I am saying only that I am having all the people assigned to your extravaganza gather at the baseball diamond to the north. As soon as I can get the bus to them and get these invading madmen contained, we will join them and depart."

"Meanwhile all the other men in the entire city will form a ring around the residential area on the south."

"Why the south?"

"The CIA men, or whoever they are, left the market and turned south."

The church door opened and several men straggled in. They carried automatic weapons and walked with the slumped shoulders of battle-weary veterans. Vulcan could sympathize with them. The attack had come so unexpectedly that in spite of drills held to handle just such a situation no one was prepared.

Vulcan sneered. "The Americans, and I am sure they are Americans, or at least they are working for the CIA, will escape through the woods long before you can put troops along the entire fringe of the forest."

"I had started closing their southerly escape early in the battle," she said.

He gritted his teeth. I'll get you yet, my sweet, he thought savagely.

The men who had just entered sensed a conflict between Vulcan and Cardwell, but she did not take advantage of the audience. She did, however, continue playing the leader role.

"Sit down, comrades," she said with easy authority. "Have our intruders left the area?" she asked.

"Negative," one man said. "They show no signs of fleeing. In the last few minutes they have set two houses on fire. I think they want to destroy the entire complex."

"Monsters," Vulcan growled. "We cannot allow three men to undo in a few hours what has taken us years to accomplish. We can rebuild, of course, but..."

"The only way you will ever be given funds and authority to rebuild is by successfully completing the next mission."

Vulcan did not acknowledge what she said. But it was true. He decided to reassert his authority and turned to the men and a few others who had just straggled in. "Where are the other unit leaders?" he asked.

"Three are moving to cover the southern escape route," Ann told him.

"Six others are dead," a man far back in the church said bitterly. "We should have been given some warning. How could such a powerful strike force get into Russia and raise such havoc here?"

"There are only three of them."

"Three? Impossible. We have suffered too many casualties."

"Just hope that there are no more than three," Ann said. "Now, have you heard the orders I gave the other unit leaders?"

Vulcan stepped in. "I have directed that the south part of town be completely cordoned off. When that has been accomplished, you will tighten the ring until the enemy have all been killed or captured."

Ann interrupted. "Take them prisoner, if you can."

Vulcan, relishing the opportunity, countermanded her instructions. "No. The mission is to kill them. If it is possible to capture one of them without opening any conceivable escape route, then you may take one of them prisoner. Now, are there any among you who do not understand the battle plan?"

At the silence that greeted his words, Vulcan looked around dramatically. "Go," Vulcan ordered. "And keep me informed."

The men left, looking a little bit more sure of themselves now that they had had at least some direction that indicated their leader wasn't without a plan.

Alone with Ann, Vulcan sat down.

"You must call our superiors," Ann said firmly.

The door eased open and Colin Edge entered, just in time to hear her remark. "We have lost all contact with the outside world. The invaders must have cut our communications," he said.

Vulcan watched Ann carefully. She blanched. Obviously she had expected to get in contact with someone before the main group left.

Vulcan pretended he had plans to nullify the lack of communications. "It is for the best. I cannot deal with bureaucrats at a time like this."

"You think all will be forgiven if the mission is successful?"

"Yes, we will have struck a blow that will hold American technology back long enough for us to catch up and surpass the West. The implications, militarily or economically are stunning."

"If you succeed," she added softly, but with a taunt in her tone.

"Oh, I will accomplish what I have set out to do." He rose and started for the side door. "In spite of you, my lovely," he added just under his breath, and a malicious gleam lit his eyes.

11

Rafael Encizo looked up from the map and turned off the flashlight they had found in the glove compartment of the car.

"We can't be more than half a mile from the town. Stop here. We'll walk."

Calvin James accepted his friend's estimate of the situation. Anyone who had lived in the mountains of Cuba during Castro's revolt against the capitalist strongman Batista, would have a sense of direction that superseded maps and compasses.

James carried out only one precaution of his own. He found a break in the woods that lined the road and drove the car across the hard narrow shoulder, then continued squeezing between the trees until there was no possibility of going farther. He wanted the car out of sight of anyone traveling the road north from Yalta. Perhaps he was being overly cautious because they had not passed another vehicle since they had taken the one he was driving from beside a comfortable-looking dacha.

Before he switched off the headlights, James sized up the area. He hoped to spot a landmark to fix the location of the car in his mind for a later escape route, should they need one. And something whispered to him that they would.

Encizo was even less optimistic. "Forget the car. It will have been reported stolen before we have a chance to use it." He started off immediately, his feet making no sound except for a snap of a broken twig. James was right behind, and they moved cautiously in the scant light provided by a stingy crescent moon.

After twenty minutes of walking blind, James finally rebelled and determinedly caught up with the man before him. "Wait." He put his hand on his guide's shoulder. "What makes you so certain we're going in the right direction? We could miss the town by miles. And what makes you think the other guys haven't already returned to Yalta?"

"Listen and you will know."

James rubbed his hand along his jaw and cocked his head as he listened. From somewhere ahead came a muffled but familiar crackling sound.

"That sounds like small arms fire. If that's the town, Katz and the guys must really be in trouble."

In confirmation, Encizo pointed to the sky. Moving to a position beside him, James saw the glow of flames dancing above the trees. Another fire burned close by the first one, but the flames were smaller and appeared to be tiring.

"The forest is too wet to burn. That has to come from the town."

"A fire. Enough shooting for a minor war."

"We must hurry," Encizo said.

With no further comment, he started through the dark forest again, avoiding trees and leaping small clumps of brush with unflagging energy, while James, less sure of himself, took longer strides to keep up.

When they finally broke free of the trees, they found themselves on a slight knoll overlooking the town. The only road ran from their left into the main street with its short lineup of businesses, many of the buildings now being consumed in flames. One of the stores set off occasional fireworks, from which they assumed it was an ammunition storage place or a gun shop.

"Well, I'll be damned." Calvin James walked another twenty yards to read the sign at the town entrance. "Cheyenne, Wyoming? That's crazy."

"Exxon." Encizo pointed at the service station with the same amazement the other three Phoenix Force members had registered when they first viewed the replica of the American town.

"McDonald's," James added. "And look at the houses. Ranches and tri-levels. A Dutch Colonial over there. And a church at the end of the street. No wonder the experts couldn't figure out what they were seeing from the spy satellites."

"Which means it's not some local version of fantasyland for kids."

"Katz and the other two must have set the fires. What do you think?"

"Look at all the people in the streets. Hell, everybody in town must be on the move. To the north it looks like women mainly, all running for cover. And to the south... Do you see what I see?"

"A lot of armed men."

"They've formed a big circle and they're tightening the noose."

Suddenly a house near the center of the circle exploded in flames, followed by a second and a third building. Three other homes were already burning.

"That's gotta be Katz and Manning. Three houses. So McCarter must still be alive." James was in the lead now, walking openly toward the edge of town. "They must be trying to level the whole town. I wonder why?"

"There's no 'why' to it. If Katz wants the place wrecked, that's the battle order for the day."

"Yeah," James agreed.

He stopped, though, when the men on the closing ring started shooting. Judging by the few tracers used and the direction of the flame spitting from the guns, it appeared the most recently lit houses were the targets.

"They keep moving and shooting like that," Encizo said, "and they're mostly going to be hitting each other."

"Not before our guys will be dead."

"Katz isn't dying when he has reinforcement on the way."

"What reinforcements?"

"You and me."

"Well, what do you want to do? Try a pincers movement? You attack from the left and I take the right."

They fell silent as they considered a plan of action because they had come as near as they dared. To get closer, they needed an aggressive strategy.

In the street, pockets of men fought the fires. But there was an Intourist bus which usually impressed tourists with its newness and cleanness, the same type of vehicle they had ridden on the morning of their arrival in Yalta. The bus rolled slowly through the main street. It turned at the church and rolled north. "Jesus," Encizo said. "You don't think there might be American tourists in that bus? Maybe we should be helping fight the fire."

"It looks to me like Katz wants the town burned..."

"Just the part on the south. There's nothing happening on the other side of the main street. So you got any ideas?"

"Yeah, we free the rest of the team, level that part of town, and get as many of the Russians as we can before we start hitchhiking back to Yalta."

"That's what I like," Encizo said. "A man with big ideas."

AS KATZ STREAKED from one burning house to another, his mind was whirring away. He remembered the aircraft he had seen when they had entered the town, and realized a possible way of escape. He motioned to his men and quickly told them his idea.

"Yeah," McCarter said. "No more than two hundred and fifty pounds. Nothing but two bucket seats, lawnmower engine, and a couple of aluminum tubes to connect the fabric-covered wing to the tail. Hang gliders with wings. They're a ball to fly."

"All right, we head for the airfield. We don't need a car to reach the airfield, but we can't head straight for it, or they'll close in on us fast."

"Do we keep burning houses on the way out?" Manning asked.

"Yes. But not in a straight line. We go out of here and start burning a larger and larger coil of houses. When we're as far from the airfield as we can get, we make a feint toward the car lot, then run like hell in the opposite direction."

"Toward the airfield?"

"It's not likely to work," Manning said.

"Of course," Katz told him, "but that's exactly what we're going to try."

12

Calvin James and Encizo approached the service station with their hands in their pockets, trying to look nonchalant.

"Keep her hard, guy," Calvin said for encouragement. "We may be burning like those houses in a minute."

"No way, man," Encizo said.

They smiled pleasantly at the armed guard who lowered his assault rifle and aimed at belly level.

"Good morning," Calvin James said pleasantly in Russian, relying on what he'd picked up from the guidebook, then asked the man if he spoke English.

The guard glared at them.

"Yes, I speak the English good," he said in a threatening tone. At fifty years of age, he was the eldest man in the program. Earlier, Arnold Vulcan had accused him of joining merely as a means of eventually defecting to the West. The charge had been mistaken then, but it had become true. He hated Vulcan and Cheyenne, hated the Communist Party and even hated Russia. He especially resented being on the fringe of the battle. If he was not truly part of the ambitious plan, he should be home with his television, he thought sullenly. "Who are you?" he demanded. "What are you doing here? You are not one of us."

He did not believe what he'd said and thought he was dealing with Vulcan's more actively involved agents, but he wanted to aggravate them.

"We're just tourists," James continued as he and Encizo moved apart slowly. "We saw the flames and came running."

"Vulcan sent you," the guard said. "To test me. I should shoot you both. He would have to say I passed the test."

"Hey, friend, wait."

"Stop. Do not move. I shoot."

Calvin James raised his hands, "Hey, don't blame us. We came to help."

"Righto, man," Encizo said. "A man who speaks good English like you should be in the United States. I know. I've been there."

"Hah," the man said. "That's impossible."

"We finish with the fire, and you can take off with us. You can be a stowaway on the ship we came in."

"Stowaway? I do not know this word."

Encizo took two steps toward the guard.

"Wait. Stand still." The man with the gun was indecisive. His gun wavered slightly as he tried to keep both of them covered.

"Relax," Encizo said, deliberately emphasizing his accent. "I am Cuban. I fought in the mountains with Fidel."

"Angola," Calvin James said. He stepped to the nearest gas pump and removed a hose. "I was trained by Russian advisers."

Encizo took a hose from another pump and raised the release lever. The indicators all moved to zero.

"Put that down," the guard said nervously, and moved in closer.

Encizo showed an open palm. "Ain't doin' nothin', guy."

From behind the guard, Calvin James raised the nozzle of one pump and squeezed the handle. A stream of gasoline squirted out, drenching the man.

He gasped from the unexpected cold shower and swung around ready to kill.

Encizo called from behind. "No *amigo*. The gasoline. It explodes. You burn."

Calvin James aimed for the Russian's face and got him full-on.

Cursing and yelling in Russian, the guard wiped his eyes with one hand to put a stop to the stinging agony.

He still had his finger on the trigger and was trying to see his target.

Calvin stepped away from in front of the muzzle.

"Careful with that gun. One spark and you're fried chicken."

"You'll die, too. You'll—"

"I think we're dead anyway. Better give me the gun."

"Nyet! Nyet."

"So shoot me, then." James put out his hand slowly and took the rifle while dousing the Russian with another shower of gasoline.

The guard bellowed something in Russian, and the Phoenix force pair recognized the anguished call for help.

"Oh-oh," Calvin James exclaimed as he spotted three Russians with guns running toward the gas station in answer to the screaming man's call.

"Think fast," Encizo said.

James did. "Step back, point the gun at our human torch as if we're holding him prisoner. Wave them up here as if we need them urgently."

The man between them had slumped to his knees and was tottering from the effect of the fumes.

"I hope you know what you're doing."

"I do."

James laid a hose on the ground and squeezed the handle, setting the holding device at the same time. A stream of gasoline poured over the concrete and down into the street.

Encizo followed suit. Before the other Russians arrived, sloshing through the stream of gasoline, the Phoenix Force detachment had four hoses going, and Calvin had entered the cashier's booth where he found the matches he needed.

Back outside, he found Encizo with three disarmed Russians drenched in gasoline. The Cuban grinned with pride. His captives, however, stared fearfully at the man now unconscious on the ground. His hands were still locked over his eyes.

"Do any of you speak English?" James asked.

"Yes," one said. "What kind of monsters are you?" he asked. "Would you really burn us to death?"

"You got it, comrade."

"Then you are with them," the Russian said, making a motion toward the south side of the town where more houses were burning. Flashes from guns showed the enemy had tightened the deadly ring considerably. In ten, fifteen minutes at the most, there would be little space left for any surviving Phoenix team members.

"Give each of them another dousing," James said.

"No. Please."

The men gagged and gasped. They were cursing and pleading in a mix of Russian and English.

"All right, let's get this straight," James said. "We all have one chance of living."

"We have?" Encizo was amazed.

James looked down the street. It was deserted. Apparently all the residents had gone to fight the other fires and to be in on the kill.

"Each of us is going to get a car and bring it back here to the station," James began giving orders. "You do just as you're told, and you will get out of this with your lives and your eyesight. Got it?"

The three nodded.

Under the watchful muzzles of their own confiscated guns they followed orders.

When they had the five vehicles in the station, they flooded the rear seats of four with gasoline from the pumps. All of them shivered with fear, and even Encizo showed signs of nervousness. There were better ways to die.

"Give each of them another dousing," James said.

"No. Please," the men said, cursing and pleading in a mix of Russian and English.

They gagged and had difficulty breathing.

Then the Russians obediently shed their shirts and undershirts and watched Calvin soak them. The underwear was then draped over partly opened windows to act like delayed action fuses of the gasoline soaked interiors.

They drove off in a convoy, feeling very cautious and as though they were driving through mines.

Calvin James drove the center car, the one that had not been flooded with gasoline. Two of the Russians drove separate cars at James's left. Encizo drove the car on the far right and controlled the Russian in the remaining car. Both Phoenix warriors kept a gun pointed out the window at their captives.

Once inside the south end of town, James climbed to the hood of his own vehicle and surveyed the battleground like a general. He immediately assessed the situation.

The circle had tightened to less than three blocks in diameter. The Russians had apparently paused, plotting their final assault or perhaps considering a surrender offer.

The occasional gunshots from inside the circle revealed the exact location where Katz, Manning and McCarter were trapped. They were between two trilevel houses that had not been touched by fire.

James gave orders as if he were certain that his plan would work.

He parked his own car at the end of the alley that ran through the Russian lines and behind the house where Katz and the others appeared to be holing up for their last battle.

Two cars were at the end of the two streets that paralleled the alley. The same was true on both sides of James's position.

A slight incline worked in James's favor, but he ordered the Russians to put the vehicles in first gear and straighten the wheels.

Although he could see the Russians resume the battle and start to move toward the center of the ring, he forced himself to take one last chance.

The gasoline flowing from the open nozzles at the station should have reached the business district by now, but obviously it had torched none of the hot spots there. Nor was there any hint how much of the remaining car lot had been flooded with the explosive fuel.

He still hoped that part of his plan would explode in a streak of flame and make further strategy unnecessary.

He had to push on, though, in case that diversion failed.

"It's now or never," Encizo called to him.

The Cuban was referring to the sudden barrage of weapons that had been unleashed by the Russians in preparation for a final assault on Katz and the others.

"Okay."

He moved quickly to the two cars on the left while Encizo took charge of his own and the one that had been driven by the third Russian.

They lit the oil-soaked shirts and undershirts.

"Okay," James shouted. "Get 'em rolling, get into the woods, and you're free."

Instantly three cars, followed a moment later by Encizo's vehicle, were rolling in first gear down the streets. The flaming oil rags streamed like flags of hell against the darkness.

James and Encizo dashed forward, intent on joining their beleaguered team, threw their weapons into the remaining vehicle and started it rolling down the alley. James drove, hunching at dash level even when the car bumped into things along the way.

The first cars were nearing the Russian lines, and the mobile torches distracted the men with weapons.

Several of them raised their hands, trying to indicate that the drivers should halt their vehicles.

But the cars kept moving, and Calvin James started a silent chant, willing that things should start happening. "Blow, blow, blow."

Encizo raised his head so he could see out the window. "Maybe it's not going to work."

"It has to."

Ahead, the battle had reached its final phase. As if it were controlled by a drawstring, the perimeter diminished by the second.

"Come on, blow. There are enough fumes inside those cars to make one hell of a bang even if the tanks don't explode."

"You ever tried this trick before?"

"No."

"Then it is pure theory."

"Hell, that's right. And I'm counting on luck, too."

"If you got any more ideas, let's use them now."

"I'm saving a couple for later."

"There isn't going to be any later. Here come three guys to check us out."

James didn't bother to raise his head. He positioned his rifle so he could shoot the first man to stick his face close to the door window, but that was where his plans ended. He might kill a few more Russians before he died, but what then? He could see no way out. Not for himself, and not for Phoenix Force.

13

Death was the ultimate flaw in the magnificent human body, Yakov Katzenelenbogen thought philosophically as he looked out from his tiny corner formed by a concrete planter on one side and the house on the other. Actually, makeshift though it was, his shelter offered good protection. The Russians had come up with a supply of grenades from somewhere, but the overhang of the house roof rendered them ineffective.

He lay on his belly, hoping that Manning and McCarter were still alive at the front of the two houses. If they were not, though, it didn't make all that much difference, he thought in consolation of himself, because they would all die soon in any case.

Katz had stationed himself at that spot in the back, looking across the alley to the houses beyond, because of the small trees there that he had wanted to turn his thoughts to at the moment before he would stop thinking entirely.

Actually, the largest tree was nearly barren, and its remaining leaves were like sieves from the bullets.

Man should let trees decide when it was time to shed their leaves, he thought. And men should let others die in their own time.

Often that wasn't possible, but perhaps he had chosen his own time by coming here in the first place.

And it was not a bad place to die.

The enemy seemed incapable of hitting him. The end depended on the ammunition he had carried to this place.

He had no idea how many shells remained in any given weapon except for one Russian assault rifle. That one was completely full. He was saving it for the last, which would not be long in coming.

Some of the Russians were advancing as they fired, their slugs chipping away at his little fort. An open wound dropped blood to his shoulders from a shallow furrow across the top of his head.

"Manning?" he called, although it brought a new storm of bullets aimed in his direction.

"Yeah."

Katz smiled wryly. Still alive.

"David?"

"Here," McCarter replied, and Katz marveled. It was a victory that they were all still alive.

Time to take more Russians with them, he thought. The creed of the hero and the fanatic.

Had his undaunted determination to destroy the town cost the team their chance to live? If he had returned to Yalta before they had engaged the Russians, he could have told Hal Brognola what they had found. Cheyenne, a masterpiece for training deep penetration agents.

Now the three of them would be dead. Brognola would have to send others to complete the mission and find out what had happened. Nagging at his conscience even more was a question Katz feared he would never have answered before he died.

What had happened to Calvin James and Rafael Encizo? Katz would have preferred to die thinking that the backup pair was still safe and alive in Yalta. That would have been comforting. Not only would their lives be saved; they would also form the nucleus of a new Phoenix Force.

But he was whistling "Dixie." They had the battle plan. Orders called for them to remain in Yalta until it became apparent that Katz and his detachment were not returning within the deadline, but they would not have waited any longer than required.

No. They were here somewhere. Beyond the Russians, either dead or alive, the black and the Cuban would have made their attempt at a rescue.

I asked too much of my men, he told himself. Ten to one they were dead, heroes whom no one would ever honor.

"Ah, well," he sighed. He had thought of death and honor and dishonor enough. "Get back to work," he told himself aloud, and found that the self-administered advice was well-timed.

A Russian had climbed to a roof across the alley. He was at the peak, steadying himself for a killing shot, probably hoping to catch Manning or McCarter from above and behind them.

Katz took up one of the weapons he had cached in his makeshift bunker.

It was a Mega Dart Gun, an MX-7 powerful enough to fire a variety of .40-caliber darts at a velocity of 720 per second. The one he had taken off a corpse had a camouflaged metal finish.

It was not meant to be a man-killer by any means, but if he could catch the sniper in the face or upper torso, the man would be out of action. The benefit to Manning and McCarter could mean an extra thirty seconds of life and Katz would not open himself up to the withering barrage the advancing enemy would unleash if they saw the flash of a gun.

He inserted a long wire dart into the chamber. It had power enough to penetrate body armor made of ballistic nylon. Then he closed the bolt and locked it by drawing back the handle on the side. The clicking sound assured him the bolt was properly seated. He attached the metal stock and pressed the butt against his shoulder as he looked down the sight tube. Making slight adjustments for wind and elevation, he drew back on the elastic power handle until it clicked into place.

He aimed, pulled the trigger and heard the dart hiss through the air.

The missile slammed home; the Russian jerked backward, firing into the air, and then rolled down the roof and thumped to the ground. That single shot confused the encircling wolf pack. One of their own had been hit, and they had neither seen nor heard the responsible weapon. Their final advance halted.

"Great!" Katz exclaimed.

He grabbed for more darts. He fired at those closest to him. Four dropped away like figures in a shooting gallery.

Another triumph. A small one. Another delay of the inevitable.

He fired the last of the darts, got his targets, and saw them replaced by reinforcements. Was there no end to the enemy supply of bodies?

The Russians were pushing forward again behind the withering hail of lead they unleashed.

Katz returned fire with a last desperation as bullets chipped the planter to his side. Dirt sprayed into the air, and chips of concrete stung his cheeks.

They were just across the alley now and also closing in from both sides. He could not hold them off, had no hope of returning fire measure for measure.

Abruptly the advance stopped, and Katz spotted a car rolling slowly down the street.

Beyond that he saw two other cars, one twenty or more feet behind the first. The third was even farther back. Together the vehicles reminded him of a strange funeral procession. There were no lights, just some flares at the top of the window on each of the vehicles.

Peering cautiously over his sanctuary, he discovered two more cars were rolling along the streets to the south.

Several Russians broke ranks to check the first car, trotting alongside, using it as a shield. It obviously seemed safer to them than making the final plunge.

An explosion dissolved the darkness. Slivers of the car's metallic body became embedded in the bodies of the men nearest the vehicle, sculpting deep, ragged holes in their faces. Some of the projectiles rained down around Katz's shelter.

The vehicle rolled along, its interior engulfed in flames. It had advanced beyond the house where the Phoenix Force leader had made his last stand.

A similar explosion came from the street behind him, where Manning and McCarter dug their heads under protective tents of arms and elbows.

The fuel tank of the first vehicle went off with a roar that deafened and a flash of flame that blinded. The car disintegrated, its metal fragments turning bodies into ribbons of flesh. Burning tires sizzled and whirled and hissed, and down on the ground rained glass, blood and broken bodies in a glistening carnage that came straight from hell.

"Katz," McCarter called. "You all right?"

The answer was lost in the explosion of another car only half a lot away from him. It had the same devastating effect on the Russians. They ran, they screamed, they died. Some were bathed in the flaming gasoline and were unlucky enough to die slowly.

The third and fourth cars, too, fulfilled Calvin James's plans.

Flashing fireballs inside the vehicles were followed by still more murderous explosions when the fuel tanks went up. Russians were lifted off their feet and flung against buildings. Those not killed or wounded, dived for cover. Katz picked some of them off.

He never enjoyed killing but there was satisfaction in destroying those who meant to kill him. Were there time, he would have pondered the origin of the incendiary brigade. But he was too busy and simply took advantage of it.

Immediately after the last two explosions, Katz heard a familiar voice.

"Katz, get in. Hurry."

He looked around to see where the voice was coming from and saw that the Russian survivors were trying to get away from the fifth vehicle before it, too, became a deadly fireball. Katz, though, saw the right door swing open.

"Get in. Hurry."

He saw no one in the car, but he knew the voice.

"Manning, McCarter, this way. Hurry, dammit."

They came running without any cover.

"Get in," Katz told them.

"James! Encizo!" Manning exclaimed, very happy to see them. McCarter squeezed into the rear seat with the Cuban and the Canadian. He rolled down the window, and thrust out the muzzle of the Mitchell Arms AK-22 he was carrying.

Katz took the front seat.

"Go in!" he yelled.

The car lurched forward as James veered off the blocked alley and cut across the grass between two houses. They cleared the scattered line of the enemy before any of the Russians realized the car was being driven by the escaping foreigners.

Immediately bullets began whizzing in the car's direction.

"Bonnie and Clyde," McCarter laughed in exultation. He braced the Mitchell and sprayed a group of marksmen who had lined up in the kneeling position, trying to get off a last volley before the enemy disappeared from sight. But the speeding vehicle cut them down like bowling pins before they could fire a single shot.

"Head for the airfield," Katz shouted. He pointed in the direction of the clearing behind the church.

"You got a plane coming in to take us out?" James said hopefully.

"Three of them," McCarter said.

"Three?"

"Ultralights."

"You mean those things that look like they were built in 1901?"

"You got it, partner. Our wings to freedom."

"You're the pilot. Can we all get on one of those toys?" Encizo asked with doubt.

"No. Two, max. You go with me. Katz, you take Calvin. Gary, you get your own plane."

"What the hell do I know about flying one of those things?"

"You're going to get a lesson right now. So listen, and listen good."

"You can't expect me to learn that way."

"The Wrights got less help before they went up. Besides, you'd take the controls practically from the start even if you were getting formal lessons. These aren't 747s. Stick forward on taxiing, stick back on takeoff. Stick and pedal left for a left turn."

"I'd never be able to land one of those winged baskets. Neither would Katz."

"If you're lucky, there'll be a parachute fastened on the top of the wing that brings you and the plane down easy."

"But where are we going to come down?"

"Ask Katz."

They were planning too far in advance, they realized when a wall of gun-wielding men came into their sight.

"Everybody down but me," Katz ordered.

Even James ducked his head and the old Phoenix leader leaned from the window and blazed away until his weapon clicked on empty. He dropped it out the window and took up a Calico High Tech .22 that Manning had brought aboard.

A line of bullets stitched across the windshield, leaving patches of cracked glass at ten inch intervals. From off to the left, a wiser group of defenders went for the tires.

Katz felt the curse of finality again. In moving to return the fire from this new direction he saw men rushing toward the car lot. If one of our tires blow on our car, Katz thought, then we're back where we started. Trapped again.

At that moment there was a roar and flames erupted in the main street gutter in the center of the business district and streaked toward the lot.

"We opened the pumps at the station," James said with a note of pride in his voice.

The flames reached the car lot, rising skyward like quick-growing weeds until they were three stories high. The explosions started slowly, then increased in tempo until it was like a string of firecrackers popping and hopping about on a sidewalk at a Fourth of July celebration.

The massive fire was just too much and made the fight go out of the Russians.

Many of them dropped their weapons and tried to get out of the city in any direction they could.

The Phoenix team cheered. They thought they had it made. In minutes they would be airborne.

The mood was suddenly broken. "Stop," Katz ordered sharply.

Calvin James looked aghast, but drove the brake pedal to the floor.

The car went into a skid, but Katz was out of it before it stopped.

Only then did the others see the unbelievable: an Intourist bus turning a corner from the undamaged north residential side of town.

"Where the hell are they going at a time like this?" Katz asked.

His answer was a barrage of bullets that buzzed all around him.

"Let's forget it, Katz," Gary Manning yelled. "Let's get out of here alive."

Katz hesitated, then ducked and swung into the car as it leaped ahead.

For a moment there was relative quiet as they raced to the airstrip.

Now if I don't kill myself trying to fly a kite, Katz thought to himself, maybe I'll see the dawn one more time at least.

14

Inside the Intourist bus, Arnold Vulcan stood at the front as it rolled carefully through the smoldering ruins of Cheyenne. The driver swerved repeatedly to miss the dead and the dying.

The flames had begun to consume the north section of the city. People were saving their personal belongings. A few half-heartedly poured water on the flames with garden hoses.

To the south the flames had taken on the ferocity of an escaped tiger. He refused to look in that direction.

Vulcan felt nothing for the injured, the dead, or the homeless. They had brought it upon themselves. None of them had fought hard enough or wisely enough.

He had one concern. He must be out of the country before anyone in a high position learned about the catastrophe.

Vulcan still found it difficult to believe that so much carnage had been wreaked upon his beloved dreamworld in a matter of hours. And all the slaughter had been carried out by only five men, although he received reports that a full company, a platoon at least, had ravaged his domain.

The men with burned clothing and smeared faces had reported to him with awe in their voices.

"There were so few of them," one after another had said.

"Yet it seemed they were everywhere." The phrase was repeated like a scratched record, over and over.

"And so many of you," Vulcan replied in disdain.

"We could shoot, but they were always well covered."

"They changed positions so often."

"They were behind us when we thought we had them encircled."

"We could do nothing."

Except get in each other's way, Vulcan thought.

"You taught us that one or two well-trained men or women can do more damage than divisions of soldiers."

Vulcan believed that. His entire Cheyenne was based on that theory. It was particularly true in peacetime, when ponderous armies and doomsday weapons were useless. The great powers dare not show their real strength for fear of setting off a worldwide holocaust.

He still trumpeted about that the Three Mile Island incident was a massive victory his people had achieved. Actually he could not prove that his graduates deserved credit for the nuclear disaster. Afterward, though, the Politburo funded the construction of his ambitious training grounds.

Since then his graduates had achieved key positions throughout the American nuclear power system. Current orders forbade them to unleash any catastrophic explosions, but they plagued the industry so successfully that the American media and conservationists bannered the slightest incident. The growth of the nuclear power industry ground to a halt in America; the enemy became more dependent upon Middle East oil, a supply the Communists could disrupt easily whenever need be.

The Cheyenne project gloried in other successes. Vulcan's people masterminded labor strikes that disrupted the American balance of trade. They ran drugs into military bases in the States and around the world.

Their accomplishments were many, and the sphere of their operations was extensive. The Politburo would remember his successes.

These comforting thoughts, balm to his current wounds, were interrupted when Colin Edge signalled the bus to stop in front of the computer store.

Vulcan's prime assistant had soot on his face, and his clothes were bloodied. He had served as Vulcan's eyes through the night's battle.

He had his luggage in hand and discarded a gun on the sidewalk before he climbed in.

"You must clean yourself up before we reach Yalta," Vulcan chastised him.

"Yes, sir," Colin Edge agreed meekly before telling more important matters in a whisper only meant for his superior's ear. "The attackers are escaping by using the Ultralights."

Vulcan swung about. His eyes flared with anger. The planes had been Ann Cardwell's suggestion. She said they would be a good sport for his agents. Not only would the small aircraft give his people a club to join, they could be useful in surveillance. No one would shoot down such a harmless-looking aircraft should it stray over a military installation.

Ah, blame her for the escape, he thought. His genius lay in his ability to turn fault to advantage.

"Is no one stopping them?"

"Some tried," Colin Edge said. "I think the enemy is escaping anyway, but how far can they go?"

"Not far," Vulcan admitted. "Forget the invaders. They will be a minor irritation if we succeed in what we are about to do."

He returned all his attention to the people on the bus. He waited for them to quiet.

"I can now tell you your mission."

He had their attention.

"As you were briefed in the beginning, you are supposed to be an ordinary group of Americans from all over that country, which has been touring Russia by bus. You know little about the other travelers except for your husband, wife, or companion. If you have been circumspect as ordered, only Colin, Miss Cardwell, and I know your fabricated life story. Without arousing suspicion, reveal as little as possible about where you came from in the States. But if it becomes necessary to lay somebody's suspicion to rest, then do not be afraid of revealing anything we have implanted in your biography."

"We know all that," the man named Larson interrupted.

Vulcan ignored him.

"For this, the second half of your extended holiday, you will take a Greek cruise ship sailing early this morning. Actually, the ship is already waiting for us in Yalta. Your major stops will include Istanbul, Athens, Mykanos—the most beautiful of all the Greek Islands—and finally, Venice, Italy."

The bus buzzed with excited voices until a man named Morgan interrupted. For months his part in the project called for practicing welding.

"Do you mean we are going to continue in spite of the disaster this evening?" he asked.

"Would you prefer to remain behind?" Vulcan asked.

"No. No," he answered quickly, too quickly, and people laughed nervously.

None of them care for anyone else, Vulcan thought. Why should I care what happens to any of them?

"Wait. Does this mean we are not going to the United States?" a woman asked. She was an experienced secretary.

"Heavens, no," Ann Cardwell spoke up. She sat down on a front aisle seat while Vulcan remained standing. "You will continue on to your homes in the States where you will be helped to set up new lives by a field commander."

Vulcan took charge again. "Remember the résumé of your American life at all times."

"I am supposed to be a recovered alcoholic," Larson said.

A woman added, "And I am supposed to be a call girl."

"Yes. We use those backgrounds frequently," Ann Cardwell said.

"Stop it," Vulcan intervened. "I just told you not to reveal anything about yourself, even to each other, unless it is necessary." He knew there were informers among them, and already they had all revealed too much. He did not really care, but the fear of being caught breaking rules gave him a leverage over them that he needed. "Believe me, your artificial life has been assembled by experts. We have never had a casualty due to an identity problem."

"All right," Larson said. "What about the cruise?"

"What about it?"

"Why are we the only group ever scheduled to travel in such luxury?"

"You are the largest group we have ever sent out."

"Bullshit, as the Americans say. There is a secret reason behind this. This I know."

"You will be briefed aboard ship," Vulcan said. His voice was growing angry.

"Bullshit again. We have agreed, all of us, that we will not leave Russia without knowing the fundamentals of our mission."

"The cruise is mere transportation," Colin Edge spoke up, something he rarely did with Vulcan at hand.

Larson sneered at him. "We do not believe that. We are certain we have a mission aboard ship."

There had been a leak, Vulcan realized. "We?" he mocked. "Since when do you speak for others, Larson?"

A man halfway down the bus answered. "Since tonight. Since we saw other trainees gunned down in the street, since we watched strangers destroy half of your Cheyenne."

Another agreed. "Yes, Larson speaks for all of us."

"Agreed."

Others chimed in, and there was a chorus of support.

"Yes."

"We will not board without knowing."

Vulcan looked out the window. There were lights in houses lining the road, indicating that they were in the outskirts of Yalta. He had intended to hold firm to his rules, but it looked as though he would have to yield to some extent.

The rebellion drove him to a frenzy. He wished he could redirect the bus to a KGB establishment he knew about and get revenge for the insubordination.

If there was any chance whatsoever that he could strike the same target at a later date, he would have done just that. But that was impossible, nor could he form a new team in time.

"You know this borders on treason," he said.

No one spoke. He had cowed them temporarily, yet he knew he had to let them know something, or they might become rebellious and unreliable at a later time when he could least afford it.

"You are going to sink the cruise ship," he said.

"What?"

The single exclamation spoke for the entire group.

Ann Cardwell raised her hands for silence. "Don't worry. Your safe escape is all arranged. We can't afford to lose any of you. Reverend Vulcan and I will be aboard, also."

"Me, too," Colin Edge added.

"Yes, Colin will be with us. We don't have any desire to commit suicide. You will be perfectly safe."

Vulcan allowed Colin and Ann to reassure the people and give him more time to recover from his rage, which he could barely control.

"How can we possibly sink a ship?" a woman asked.

"Larson should know."

All heads turned in Larson's direction.

It seemed that some kind of understanding had dawned in his mind, and apparently he was satisfied. It seemed as though suddenly his stature had grown within the group, and he savored the glory coming to him.

Vulcan finally continued. "In your luggage we have placed all the hand weapons you will need. In your toilet articles and elsewhere in your suitcases, each of you is carrying a quantity of commercially available chemicals, which Larson, with some of you helping him, can quickly blend into C-4 plastic, nitroglycerin, PBN-1, Astrolite A-1-5. As he can tell you, some of the concoctions he can make are the most powerful non-nuclear explosives in use today. You will not find it difficult to follow his instructions."

A woman tried to speak up, and Ann answered her unspoken question. "After the regular fire drill required the first day at sea, you will be contacted. The next sound of the warning whistle will be for real. In this ship, regulations call for passengers to gather in the lounges. You will head straight for your boats. You'll be safely away from the ship before the explosions."

"So don't worry," Vulcan said. "Soon you will be aboard one of the finest ships sailing today."

He sat down and looked out the window to relax. The night was dark although it wouldn't be for long. The streets were quiet except for the drone of engines.

Strange. He could see no moving vehicles to the front or to the sides.

He felt chilled suddenly.

The engine noise was coming from above.

THE CAR HAD LEAPED onto the airfield, its left front tire punctured by a lucky shot from a Russian sentinel at the edge of the strip.

The car struck the Russian, and his body bounced upward, then dropped across the hood, obscuring the driver's vision. But James did not let up on the accelerator. Only when they were alongside the featherweight aircraft did he lock the brakes and skid to a stop.

On the mad dash from the smoldering town, David McCarter, who was checked out on propeller craft up to four engines, had described the Ultralights and their simple operation.

At the field, Katz sent Encizo and James to take up a holding position. Their assignment was to provide cover for the others, so they could become acquainted with the aircraft on which their escape depended.

Finally there was no more time for "flight training." The townsmen were still a real threat and could literally arrest their flight at any moment.

The engines were running. McCarter was at the controls on the right flank, strapped into the tiny bucket seat. The back of the seat was a curved, six-inch long by four-inch tall aluminum backrest. It was attached to the front mounts for the small, pusher-type engine.

A stick, two foot pedals, and a throttle constituted the controls. The instrumentation amounted to no more than a plastic tube with a hole at the bottom. A button in the middle of the tube rose or fell in ratio to the speed of the wind. It was good enough for gauging takeoff and stall speeds. It was adequate, too, for judging appropriate landing speed, though they would not need that capability.

They knew from the start that they would be using the explosive-deployed parachutes when they finally came down.

In the center aircraft was Katz. He did not worry so much about trashing himself, but he felt responsible for Calvin James who occupied the seat beside him. Before he could strap himself in, they were moving.

Manning and Katz pushed the throttles forward to keep abreast of McCarter. They were learning by actually having to do what they couldn't fully know how to do. Many others had learned the same way in the early days of the sport.

Nobody tried to see the speed indicator in the dark. When the Briton pulled back on his stick, the fragile craft started to climb smoothly.

Katz hauled back too hard, felt the engine falter and came down again with a teeth-cracking bump that damaged the fragile landing gear on the right. He pushed the throttle farther forward, lifted the right wing slightly and started a one-wheel takeoff.

He veered toward Manning, then overcontrolled to the right. The plane seemed weightless, and it bounced about in the air, with the tail intent on doing its own thing.

Katz almost wondered if the controls had any effect on the craft's capricious behavior. Being on the ground getting shot at from three directions paled by comparison.

"Hey, Katz," Calvin James called as he clung to a strut with both hands. "Katz."

"Don't bother me. I'm busy."

"The trees—"

"Oh, hell!" The trees were directly ahead of them.

Katz ignored the niceties of level flight and drew back on the stick, restraining the instinct to haul back as far as he could.

They cut through the small branches of the trees that clutched the landing gear. The very tips swiped at the legs of the fliers.

The nose dipped, and Katz corrected, then climbed at a forty-five degree angle. The craft started to stall.

He needed sixty feet to recover, according to McCarter.

He put the nose down and assessed the situation. He jutted his chin forward in determination and opted for a bank to their left. When he spotted a slight depression in the trees, he headed in that direction.

James saw Gary Manning's fragile craft directly above the same indentation. His ship appeared to be waiting.

Katz recovered from the stall, collected a few more twigs on the tail wheel, and managed to climb up under the other Ultralight, leaving two or three feet to spare.

Slowly the Israeli gained speed and slid out from under Gary Manning. The cheerful, optimistic expression that helped his men through many crises began to return to his features. Fifty feet above the trees and flying level, Katz turned to his passenger and grinned.

"Better than a roller coaster," he said.

James disagreed. "Like hell. Just get me down."

Katz, though, was beginning to enjoy the flight. When the opportunity came, he took the lead and motioned for the others to follow him.

He saw what he wanted.

A few horse-drawn wagons and one heavy truck were the only sign of life on the highway until the Intourist bus pulled onto the regular road from the entrance lane to Cheyenne.

Several miles ahead, flashing lights signaled a roadblock. That was probably the police looking for the two men who demolished so many vehicles.

Katz directed his wingmen to pull away from the road until the bus had cleared the roadblock.

Later, where the road made a broader bare swath through the forest, Katz eased down until he was flying no more than thirty feet up. James clutched the strut with both hands, but Katz ignored the danger.

Only when he had satisfied himself that he was trailing the right bus did he climb again. In the city, following the bus became more difficult, although the relatively empty streets helped.

The port was just ahead, and James yelled in warning. "Radar. The Russians will pick us up on radar any second if they haven't already."

Katz disagreed. "We're too low."

He did a wing-over and came back, skimming a freighter on one side of the longest pier. On the far side, forklift trucks were moving luggage into a brilliantly lit cruise ship.

The bus from Cheyenne stopped at the covered walkway to the sparkling white ship with Greek markings.

Katz made one last low pass. He saw the ship's name. The *Odyssey*. That was all he needed. He headed out to sea with every eye on the wharf watching him and the other two aircraft.

They flew twenty feet above the water in an attempt to keep from being detected by radar.

Once he accepted that his feet were not going to drop into the surf, Calvin took on a new worry. "Now what, Katz? We're going to have MiGs on our tails any minute."

"We need a boat," Katz said.

"What kind of boat?"

"Anything as long as it's within swimming distance from where we dunk these things."

"And precisely where are we going to do that?"

"Some place before we run out of gas."

Accomplished frogman that he was, Calvin James wasn't happy. He shouted over the small engine that was disproportionately loud for its size. "I don't see any ships out here. Things are still very iffy, aren't they?"

Katz looked at him. "I think we have accomplished something close to a miracle already. After all this trouble, our luck just has to hold out. We will report to Stony Man Farm yet! And this is our best chance."

James mumbled to himself. "Yeah, man. And if not, what a way to go!"

15

The three Ultralights circled the small freighter, closing in around her until the fragile wingtips threatened to touch the ship's radio antenna. The skipper cut power. She went dead in the water.

He guessed correctly. The birds were signaling distress.

He watched in disbelief as a loud popping sound launched a tethered white object flying straight up from each plane. Three parachutes bloomed. He put a dinghy over the side and sent his crew about the business of collecting the floating aviators. Their crafts began to sink slowly into the Black sea.

It was a part of the world Katz remembered his father talking about with pleasure.

Seven hundred and fifty miles long, the Black sea formed a large part of Russia's southern border and was the only coastline for Communist Romania and Bulgaria. To the south was West-leaning Turkey, once the heart of the Ottoman empire that had controlled the Middle East and southeastern Europe.

Turkey still controlled the Bosporus, the Black sea's only exit to the Mediterranean.

If the freighter were headed there, Katz calculated that there would be no trouble. If it had departed Yalta for one of the other Communist ports, he was prepared to take the ship by force. The five warriors came aboard carrying the AK-47s and a pistol or two tucked in each of their belts, and the crew backed away in fear of the tattered, battle-ravaged blood-stained strangers climbing up the rope ladder.

The captain appeared at the door to the bridge and shouted in a language that Katz did not understand. In response, Katz asked, "Do you know English? French? Russian?"

"English will do," the captain said with a heavy accent. He was a short, thick-bodied man with olive skin and wiry gray hair. "Are you pirates? Do you intend to take the ship?" Despite the questions that seemed to indicate that he expected the worst, the captain appeared to be unnaturally calm.

Katz sensed that there was a danger of misunderstanding. "Where are you bound?" he asked evasively.

"Istanbul."

As a peaceful gesture, Katz put his rifle on the deck where crates stacked high covered the hatches and everything stored below.

"Put your rifles down, too," Katz instructed his men.

The captain accepted his visitors' token act of goodwill by stepping into the open and leveling an automatic weapon at them. Two other armed men appeared at the stairway to the other side of the bridge.

McCarter cursed, but Katz held up his hand warningly. He knew that at any moment his men would leap for cover and a violent firefight would erupt. But one or more of them might end up paying with their lives for going up against automatic rifles already pointed in their direction.

"We were escaping Russia," Katz said.

The captain laughed. "In those things? Better you should sail the Atlantic in my skiff." He lowered his weapon and made a sweeping motion with his hand. "Come up. All of you. We must get under way. And bring your guns. I boast too much when I think anyone would want to take my old ironside wife."

All along the deck of the small ship, the crew relaxed and nodded with welcoming smiles, following the captain's lead.

"Of course, if the Russians come for you, I will say you are pirates who overpowered my crew and me."

On the bridge, the captain turned on more lights although the sun reddened the eastern sky to their stern. He was the typical craggy master seen around the world aboard rusting trucks of the sea. If he had a nationality, he had no doubt severed his relationship in favor of citizenship in his own floating domain.

"Let's see, what do we have here?" He looked at Gary Manning. "An American, yes."

Gary was emphatic. "No." Like most citizens of a country overshadowed by superpower neighbors, he was fiercely proud of his homeland. "Canadian."

"Ah, yes. And you," he said to McCarter. "A limey, yes?"

"You bloody well better believe it."

"And you, Russian?"

"Israeli," Katz said quickly. "Well, I spring from Jews in Russia."

"A good place to spring far away from. And an African," he continued.

"No. American through and through," Calvin James corrected him.

"Cuban," Encizo hurried to inform the curious man. "The non-Castro kind."

"A veritable United Nations," the captain continued as he interspersed his conversation with orders in several languages addressed to his crew members getting the ship moving again. "You must all be CIA or MI5, perhaps KGB disguised to trap a poor seaman who plies the open seas. Do not answer. You would lie. Everyone lies these days; it is the plague of the twentieth century."

Katz interrupted. "You work these waters regularly?"

"If there is cargo that no one else wants to carry. Yes. If not, I sail anywhere."

"Do you know the cruise ship in the harbor at Yalta?"

"Know her well. I look across at her berthed at the best pier in all Russia. I think, that could be me in whites with braid on my cap and rich old women swooning to have a dance with me so they can tell their neighbors back home how the captain tried to seduce them and would not take no for an answer. His is a caviar life. But I talked to the captain once, and he has tired of caviar and cherries jubilee. He longs for the stew he fondly remembers from his youth as a third officer of a junk not much better than my own."

"Of course you know her name."

"The *Odyssey*. That name must have graced a thousand ships since Homer wrote his tale of one man's wanderings so many centuries ago. Perhaps I should give my own ship such a name. I am not unlike the adventurous Odysseus. The skipper of that great white beauty travels the same course over and over again. I go where I wish."

"What is the *Odyssey*'s itinerary?" Katz asked, using his last reserves of strength. He wanted to get the information he needed from the wiry old skipper and then get some sleep for himself and his men.

"From Venice to Greece, Istanbul, and Russia. Then he retraces his own wake. That would never do for me, even if the adoring women passengers were young and lithesome, which most are not."

"It is faster than your ship?" Manning asked.

"When the passengers sleep and the seas are calm, yes."

"Is there any way we can get ahead of her?" Manning asked.

"She will stop to give the passengers a train ride into Romania. So we will be in Istanbul before them. Is she the reason you carry guns? I do not know that I can allow my ship to help rape such a beauty."

"You can keep the guns when we reach Istanbul. We would never get them ashore, in any case."

"Then go below," the captain said. "Find one of my men who speaks a little English or French or whatever you can understand. He will give you hot food—no caviar, of course—and dry clothing. You can sleep in the bunks of the men who are on watch. You will be well rested when we reach Istanbul."

We will need to be well rested, Katz thought. They would somehow have to interfere with the Russians whom they had seen boarding the cruise ship. He didn't know the reason for such deep undercover tactics, but it was clear to him that they were masquerading as Americans with some very important objective in mind. He just felt in his bones that a lot was at stake for America.

16

Hal Brognola sat alone in the Stony Man Farm War Room and looked again at the pictures taken by spy satellites several days before.

He felt the same apprehension in his stomach.

There was no doubting what the photos showed. Flames had consumed half of the small village he had sent his men to check. The photography experts had circled small dots. "Bodies," they told him. "A lot of bodies."

What about his men? he wondered. How had such a simple mission gone so awry?

He blamed himself for not being emphatic enough. The mission did not warrant a risk of life, and he knew Katz had good judgment in such things.

It wasn't like Katz to overreact. Nor was it like him to stay out of contact with Stony Man for so long. Without success, Brognola had tried every communications link he knew, including an open telephone call to the Hotel Yalta.

All he knew was that a battle had engulfed the mysterious Russian village. The latest computer-enhanced photos showed trucks and vans moving in to take away the dead and the injured and to begin cleaning up the debris.

Washington pressured Brognola, too. The President wanted to know what had gone wrong. Where was the Phoenix team? Where was their report?

"Send in someone else," the White House said. "If the burning of that village is laid on our doorstep, we could be humiliated at a crucial time in our relationship with the man in Moscow."

It was always a crucial time in Moscow-Washington relations, Brognola thought bitterly.

What had happened to his men? That was his first concern.

When the phone rang, he grabbed for it as if it might spring away from his fingers. "Yes?" he said.

"It's me."

The familiar voice of Yakov Katzenelenbogen provided a relief that almost sent him soaring. But there was more to come. So cautiously he asked, "You all right?"

"Good enough."

The head Fed hated to ask the next question. "And the others?"

"Okay."

"Where are you?" Brognola realized the call had come in on a line that was not secure. Katz could be calling from a pay phone anywhere in the world. Brognola could only hope the wrong ears were not listening.

"Istanbul."

"I thought you were going to visit your old hometown."

"You mean Cheyenne, Wyoming?"

What was Katz talking about? Brognola wondered, but said nothing.

"No. I didn't get home, but the place we visited made me think of the old homestead."

Brognola was still puzzling over the reference to Cheyenne, and his mind raced, looking for clues, something that would click in.

"It was a great place to train for a rodeo."

Finally, Brognola thought he understood. The town must have been much like a small city in the States. And training? Hell, yes, he got the picture. The town was a KGB training ground for foreign agents. That explained why the team had left it in flames.

"Then you're ready to come home?" Hal asked.

"No. We'll take a few days off, a kind of odyssey."

Odyssey? A trip.

"What airline will you be flying?"

"No planes. Can't get reservations this late."

Well, you're sure not going by bus, the Fed told himself. Car? Maybe. Or a ship. Odyssey sounded like a ship's name.

While he talked, he pressed the speaker button to free his hands. He typed the name into the computer and fed in a number of commands. He had it before Katz said anything more significant.

The terminal displayed the information he was looking for. The *Odyssey*, due out of Istanbul early the next day.

"Do you need tickets?" he asked.

"Yes. They might be hard to get this late."

"That's my problem. Need anything else?"

"Yeah. Everything. We left home without American Express traveler's checks."

"Go to the American Express office. They'll have money waiting for you."

"Thanks, Dad."

"What?"

"Like a college kid," Katz said. "Calling home for money."

"Oh. Well, when can I expect you home?"

"We haven't seen the high point of the trip yet."

Hal puzzled over that one. The team had almost leveled a Russian espionage training facility, but that was not the high point of their trip?

The team should not be on a mission he did not understand. He wanted no loose cannon on the decks of his battlewagons.

"You sure that you should extend your trip? Your health isn't that good."

"That's the truth, but we hope to see some of the people we met during the first two days of our stay."

Brognola shook his head. He would get a clearer report as soon as Katz could use code, but there was no relaxing until then.

"Okay, but don't overdo. Father's orders."

"Yeah, Pop. Just don't forget the money."

KATZ INSPECTED HIMSELF and his four companions whose wrinkled clothes made them look like bums who slept on street corners.

"We're going shopping," he told his tattered group.

They left the booth and elbowed their way into the bedlam that is Istanbul.

They noticed one of the many ornate minarets, from where would come the call to the faithful to prayer. Taxis choked the streets and honked, adding to the noise of pedestrians milling about.

It was a city of many ages: modern skyscrapers and exclusive shops gave way without warning to giant marketplaces not much changed since the time of Jesus Christ. In the markets, loosely covered by sagging tarps, were hundreds, perhaps thousands of open-air shops and stalls. They created a maze that threatened to ensnarl newcomers and never set them free. Buyers could buy computer programs in one stall and bargain for pails of water in the next.

Having collected their money, they cleaned up in the hotel they had checked into. After buying clothes and luggage, the Phoenix Force crew entered the dimmest and most remote section of a large bazaar. In the eerie light, welders squatted on dirt floors to create wrought-iron ceiling fixtures. It was there that the five commandos had to shop for guns.

Reluctant Turks, wearing turbans and long shirts that reached to their shoes, forgot their fear of entrapment and arrest when the price was high enough, usually reached after a good deal of haggling. They sold guns, knives, garrotes, plus an assortment of grenades, smoke bombs, kung fu throwing stars, and a few other trinkets of self-defense. Certainly, it was one of the more fascinating places they had seen and could well imagine what some of the customers were who frequented the place.

Satisfactorily clothed and armed, they were back on the dock when the *Odyssey*'s side thrusters cozied up to her berth.

While Turkish officials were aboard clearing the ship and her passengers, the five Phoenix Force men were allowed to go aboard.

The ship they boarded was so luxuriously appointed that it seemed as if they'd entered a floating palace. The foyer was a carpeted piece of art dreamed up by an imaginative interior decorator. Curved staircases with brass railings led to decks above and below. Murals in the Impressionist style portrayed the ship's ports of call.

There were nightclubs and cozy bars, reading rooms and casinos. Swimming pools, saunas, shuffleboard courts, and rows of deck chairs were available to the passengers.

But there was an unusual feature. Everywhere, it seemed, were personal computers and network terminals. They were lined up in corridors and in waiting areas. Each had its own desk and comfortable chair. There were also terminals for mainframes in one conference room.

Katz was certain that the modems beside most of the keyboards connected with super computers in the States.

Each station was occupied by a youngish-looking man or woman, some of them looking as though they had no time for combing their hair. Often there were arguments in progress, over RAM and ROM and artificial intelligence. They all appeared so intent on the machines that they apparently had no plans to leave the ship.

But the other five hundred passengers were waiting impatiently to go ashore.

The computer conventioneers—he was sure that's what they were—didn't concern Katz. He remembered Hal Brognola telling him that the top Western brains in the computer field would be traveling and meeting in the area. But seeing them reminded the Israeli that the President of the United States would be in Venice to meet them.

Katz's mind locked in on the idea. That would explain, he thought, why the Communists got aboard the ship. By appearing to be part of the group of mainly

American experts, the Russian agents could get close to the President.

The Russians must be planning to assassinate the President, Katz thought. For a moment the idea was deposited firmly in his mind. He was positive he was right.

Then he tested his own premise.

"No," he muttered aloud. No. The preparations are too elaborate. "They're going to kidnap him," he said aloud.

Encizo heard. "What was that?"

"Nothing, nothing at all," he replied, and lapsed back into his thoughts.

Find them aboard the ship, he told himself. Neutralize them before they disembark and take a crack at the President in Venice.

Katz knew there was no time to waste. Mykanos was the only other stop before Venice. Later he would compose a coded message to Hal Brognola, warning of a kidnapping plot in Italy, but just then he wanted his men off the ship and onto the pier. The passengers had been cleared and were flooding down the gangway to tour buses, vans and taxis.

The team hurried onto the pier. "We have to spot someone from Cheyenne," Katz repeated, as a follow-up to the run-down he had just given his men. "If we're in luck, they'll still be traveling as a group."

Katz's quick eye spotted a pattern in the way the passengers were organized. Most of them were taking tour buses. A half dozen groups, though, had arranged their own transportation.

"You tail the large van," Katz told Gary Manning, "and McCarter, the next small bus." He continued until he had handed out the other assignments. He saved the largest independent group for himself.

He was haggling for price with a taxi driver while he kept an eye on the group slowly boarding the bus.

"Reverend Vulcan," one woman called in a chime-like voice from the middle of the line. "Will we be seeing the Blue Mosque while the light is still with us?"

"Yes, I'll instruct the driver, Mrs. Friday."

Reverend? Katz brought that angle into his computerlike mind. Maybe religious groups were the least likely to harbor Russian agents. The church had been a sort of center in Cheyenne.

Hadn't he heard somebody calling for Vulcan, Reverend Vulcan, at Cheyenne? Or had that just been a dying man calling for a man of the cloth? A man's loud question about the mosque took Katz's mind from the hell of Cheyenne to soft-spoken people boarding the bus.

"Can we do that?" the man asked. "Isn't it a sin for us to enter the temple of infidels?"

"We did in Russia," another man argued.

A woman at the end of the line, apparently acting as an assistant tour director said, "Well, as a matter of fact, those were Christian churches. They were Greek Orthodox cathedrals."

"Oh, Miss Cardwell, I'm so glad you could come with us," a middle-aged woman fawned.

"Yes, Ann, darling," said another. "I feel safer, knowing you have been to all these awful places."

Ann Cardwell... He knew that name, he thought, and fixed his gaze on her face. She was so beautiful and looked vaguely familiar.

Had he seen her before?

Yes, it hit him suddenly. In the Cheyenne McDonald's.

It was as simple as that. He had found the espionage group.

He wanted to call back the guys, but they were already gone. He would have to tail the bus by himself, and then it dawned on him that the woman would know him. She would remember his arm.

His mood crashed. The beautiful Ann Cardwell was a Russian agent no matter how Western her clothes, regardless of her perfect English and flawless American accent. He wished she were not KGB. He would have enjoyed getting to know her.

Then he realized she was watching him, and from a look that appeared in her eyes it was evident she recognized him.

She controlled her expression, then apparently decided there was no sense trying to bluff.

She walked briskly up to the man whom the church members had called Reverend Vulcan.

Katz slid into the cab. He tensed, ready for anything.

Vulcan, though, only nodded and continued to herd his flock into the bus.

When they were all aboard and leaving the wharf, Katz saw Cardwell watching him through the bus's rear window.

"Driver..." Katz began.

"Call me Bulent, Bulent Cuskin." The dark-haired driver had his cab filled with pictures of tourists he had taken on day-long trips in the city. He was proud of his profession. "I drive you good. Okay. See everything. Girls. Blue Mosque. Girls. Yes?"

"Just follow that bus."

The skinny Turk objected. "Bus? No. We see best. I, Bulent Cuskin, guarantee you this."

"Follow them. I don't care for sight-seeing." Katz passed forward two twenty-dollar bills. "For starters."

"Okay. No problem. The dog cannot cut his own tail. I, Bulent Cuskin, say this."

Katz tried to relax. It promised to become a long, dull day.

The bus stopped at mosques and climbed minarets while Katz waited. In a bazaar he stayed nearby as the female tourists marveled at squatting women making coat hangers from strips of wire in a few quick, deft movements of their hands.

Katz imposed a calmness on himself that he did not really feel. His clothes clung to his sweaty body, and the oppressive humidity clogged the air passages and made breathing seem like an effort.

The handsome young woman let Katz notice by almost imperceptible signs that she was aware of his presence at all times. The look she wore was like that of a woman who is interested in what advances a certain man might make toward her. It was a very aware look, and had some elemental power to it because the experienced Israeli felt a bit of discomfort, along with a sense of embarking on an amorous adventure.

He was still with them after dark when the bus began a geared-down climb up a hill overlooking the docks. They rode through narrow, winding streets of the old city to a famous tourist attraction: Tarihi Galata Kuesi, a sixteen-hundred-year-old tower of stone. It was ten stories of rock held together with crumbling mortar.

Strange, Katz thought. It wasn't a point of interest that would normally be listed on the itinerary of a church group.

A rickety, wrought-iron cage elevator took the tourists partway up, but several stories from the top, the rattling, quivering contraption gave up and left its passengers on a vacant floor.

From there guests climbed a treacherous spiral staircase where the steps grew narrowed and the handrail stopped. Near the top the steps were only a foot wide.

The women in the group made worried sounds, and he wondered curiously whether sounds of emotions could be sure clues to people's native tongues.

Anyway, he didn't know whether the entire busload of people from Russia might be staying together or if there were some tourists mixed in among them.

He laughed at himself and considered if he was tailing one Russian secretary along with twenty members of the Cedar Rapids Missionary Auxiliary.

There was a restaurant on the top floor of the tower, and it served authentic shish kebab and powerful Turkish coffee. While everybody sat down to dine, a belly dancer appeared to entertain the guests. In her enthusiasm she pressed her undulating navel against the preacher's shoulder.

Katz watched the scene from a table across the musty café. When everyone in Vulcan's group was apparently preoccupied by his discomfort, Katz looked through the windows that revealed a bird's-eye view of the city.

There was a door leading outside to a two-foot walkway that circled the entire tower at that level. The fragile low railing discouraged guests from going outside.

But when the music stopped and the diners, including Vulcan's group, began the perilous climb down the staircase, Ann Cardwell went to the doorway, considered the danger briefly and stepped out.

It was an invitation, a trap, Katz felt, but sidestepping tables he crossed the room and went after her.

She had to have gone around to the other side of the tower. He followed. By the time he reached the far side, he could guess the nature of the trap.

Ann Cardwell had gone back inside.

Katz stopped, every sense alert. Footsteps told him two men were on the balcony with him, one coming from each direction.

Looking through a window, he saw that the waiters had disappeared and the busboys were carrying away the last of the soiled dishes.

He was alone, ten stories up on a centuries-old balcony with a loose railing. At best, he could break the window with the butt of his gun.

But it was too late. The footsteps were too close.

He removed his stiletto from its concealment. His assailants were unlikely to come at him with guns. Shots would attract too much attention in the dark silent neighborhood. He had no more desire to be arrested on a weapons charge than they. Turkish prisons had reputations second only to Mexican jails.

Calling for help was no solution. Even if he threw the gun away in time, he didn't want to miss the ship by sitting in some police station, trying to explain about Cheyenne, Wyoming, in Russia and the church group that was on some terrorist-type mission.

So he inched along the window with a stiletto in one hand and his hook ready on the other side.

A surprisingly strong wind, smelling of salty water, buffeted him.

The walkway was pocked and uneven, and he stubbed his toe in a shallow pothole.

When his hand clutched the railing for support, the iron creaked and wiggled.

He looked down.

The street was empty except for the church bus. It was moving away and heading toward the ship.

From down below drifted up the sound of cats fighting and the growling of dogs disputing ownership of a bone or claiming their territory. Cats fought. Dogs barked. Trash cans rattled. The tenements and warehouses were dark. In the distance he could see the bright lights of the city and hear muffled traffic noises.

He felt alone and isolated, but not afraid. He had survived much more treacherous situations, he told himself, but the mere simplicity of the current predicament worried him. By inching his way in one direction he could hope to engage only one of his two adversaries at first. If he stood in place, they could close in on him simultaneously.

The wind nudged him. The sickle moon succumbed to cloud cover. He would not be able to see the little movements that would give away an assailant's intentions.

He was halfway around the tower. From his left came the faint sound of crumbling concrete. The sound was no more than six feet away.

Katz stopped.

He had made a mistake. By assuming both men would be moving, he had ignored the better offense.

One of the American impersonators had stood still. The other had herded him into a trap.

Katz pressed his stomach against the glass. He wanted to forget the height and the low railing. The stiletto and his artificial hand would be adequate if luck was with him.

In the dark, with the wind whipping at his shirt, he scraped his knife across the glass.

The moving assailant stopped to listen.

He moved closer.

Silently, Katz shifted his body toward the man who waited. Then he scratched once more, using his hook and stretching as far as he dared.

The breeze died momentarily, as if it were waiting, too. Did he hear the breathing of the waiting man? The other man's sliding step drowned the sound.

Both of them must be little more than an arm's length from his hands. They paused; they sensed the kill.

Katz took a deep breath, knelt, and tested one of the uprights that held the top of the railing. It was not sturdy enough to satisfy him, but he heard the two men.

"Dmitri?" one said.

"Da," said the other.

Each knew the other's position. They poised for the attack.

Go for it, Katz told himself.

He clamped the stiletto between his teeth.

On his belly, he slid his feet over the edge. He hung, clutching an upright on either side. He kept his head and chest on the balcony and waited. A footstep from his left alerted him. Then there was a movement on his right.

They would meet directly above him.

They touched.

"Ah," one of them gasped.

There was no panic. Just surprise.

"Ivan?"

"Da."

They said something else. Where was the man who had been between them?

Almost immediately they realized their target had only one way to go. But the realization came a microsecond too late.

Katz reached up and grabbed one of them immediately. With his upper body still supported by the narrow balcony, he felt himself slipping. He hung on with his hook, clutched one of the men by his belt and hauled him from the path.

In an awkward kneeling position, the Russian lost his balance. He screamed as he hit the railing, which gave him momentary support. Katz forced himself to give another tug, this time catching a leg. He pulled harder, his upper torso sliding farther off the balcony floor.

The man broke through the railing, taking part of it with him.

He called for help all the way down. "D...m...i...t...r...i."

A mushy sound indicated that the ground had come up to meet him.

The concrete gave way where the upright rod had torn loose. Some of the loose crumbled mortar dribbled away from under Katz's shoulder. In a moment the entire balcony might go, he realized.

"Ivan?" the surviving Russian called with some degree of anxiety in his voice.

With his good hand, Katz took the knife from his teeth.

Something sharp scraped his arm. With an awkward forward thrust, Katz buried his knife in the dark bulk above. He drove it straight up into the lower abdomen.

The man named Dmitri screamed his agony, but he remained on his feet, bending low to slash at Katz again.

Katz dropped the stiletto, caught the attacker by the shirt and pulled.

The man flailed his arms, clutching for something to hold on to.

Momentarily he danced above Katz, showering his life's blood on his foe. Then he tumbled headfirst to the cobblestones below. But his grasping fingers and his momentum took Katz partway with him.

The leader of Phoenix Force team felt his weight shift. He slid, clawing at the concrete with the fingernails of his good hand.

Three feet of concrete gave way and all he could do was slow his fall.

His prosthetic hand still clutched the upright, and there seemed to be no guarantee it would hold.

He looked down.

A quick way to die, he thought. But he was in no hurry.

So he began calculating his survival. He swung himself like a pendulum, moving back and forth until his free hand got a finger hold on a few inches of flooring, but it crumbled under his weight.

When the mortar gave way, he placed his toes against the tower's wall.

You're getting old for this, he told himself. Yes, well, how many younger guys would still be alive? None, most likely.

A piece of mortar hit him on the head.

His toes slid from the indentations they had occupied. He fell, stopping only when his body weight stretched the straps and connecting wires that held the prosthetic arm to the rest of his body.

"Oh, hell," he said.

He quit worrying, quit thinking about the fall and went to work, fighting his way up. He put each big toe in a different indentation between the stones. His fingertips with the broken and bleeding nails probed until he found the space with the flooring gone directly above him. He could stretch until he caught the frame of the floor-to-ceiling window.

He moved upward, struggling, and moment by moment being uncertain when he would slip for good.

When at last he clambered up onto the balcony, he leaned against the window, his arms and legs quivering with fatigue. He desperately needed rest. His heartbeat drummed in his ears.

But there would be no rest, a siren below told him. He would have to be far from the tower restaurant before the authorities found the smashed bodies in the street.

"Surely we must have endured through the most difficult parts of our mission," he told himself comfortingly and hoped what he'd just said wouldn't turn out to be famous last words.

17

Faint smoke from the diesel engines wisped out of the single stack amidship. The *Odyssey*'s whistle blew once in spite of the lateness of the hour. Crewmen stood by her lines. Ropes to the gangway stretched taut as Katz crossed the wharf and slipped under the chain.

He was aching all over from his ordeal and perspired heavily in the humid air. Night offered no respite from the heat.

The young Greek officer frowned when he saw Katz reach the main deck, but he said nothing.

Cruise ships waited for no one. They kept no tabs on who went ashore nor did they take note of who returned. If you were only minutes late, you hired a speedboat to catch up. Otherwise latecomers were left to fly to the next port of call if they had the money and the necessary visas and other papers.

The few passengers who lined the railing applauded the Israeli's successful arrival, and his team members grinned with relief.

"I thought you'd bugged out on us, old chap," McCarter said.

Gary Manning's heavy brows relaxed their scowl, and he said in an aside, "We know you have a story to tell."

Encizo clapped a hand on Katz's shoulder as though he were looking for broken bones, and James cocked his head to one side worriedly. "Where have you been? Inside a cement mixer?"

Katz looked down at his frayed shirt and trousers. He was covered with a mixture of concrete dust and reddish-brown rust from the tower railing.

His good hand was scraped and bleeding.

"You think I look bad, you should see what I did to that cement mixer." He led all of them inside to the air-conditioned foyer. "I'd better get cleaned up before a junior officer takes me for a stowaway."

He turned toward the elevator.

"Hey," Calvin James said. "Aren't you going to tell us what happened?"

"Later," McCarter told him. "In his suite."

Wearing sport jackets and open-neck shirts, the team bore no resemblance to the warriors who had sacked a Russian town and escaped by relying on their wits.

They were following Katz until he stopped short of the elevator, coming up face-to-face with the tall slender beauty who called herself Ann Cardwell.

He greeted her in Russian. "Good evening."

"I beg your pardon?" she said, as though not understanding.

He repeated the greeting while he looked her straight in the eye.

"I don't speak Russian or whatever you're using," she responded after a confused stare at him, then started to put distance between them.

"You missed our rendezvous," he told her, switching to English.

She pretended ignorance. "Rendezvous? Have we met?"

"We should have. I followed you out onto the balcony with such high hopes."

"I'm afraid I don't know what you're talking about."

"Doesn't matter. But I did promise your two touring companions that I'd pass a message along to you. They said to tell you that they wouldn't be sailing tonight. They decided not to use that rickety elevator down from the restaurant."

She lost control of her expression for only a second. "I think you have mistaken me for someone else," she said.

The Phoenix Force four were shifting their attention from the woman to Katz and back again, following the exchange with interest.

They were baffled.

Katz's memory was fresh with the battle he nearly lost on the walkway outside the tower restaurant. The Cardwell woman had set him up as easily as an experienced whore setting up a mark for her pimp to mug.

Then the Reverend Vulcan approached. He put an arm across the woman's shoulder and started to ask her a question. "Did—"

Katz answered for her. "No. They didn't make it."

Vulcan concealed his surprise as he became aware of Katz's presence. "I beg your pardon?" he said.

Katz grinned, the dark skin folding into easy laugh wrinkles at the corner of his pale eyes. "Is that the standard response you teach at Cheyenne?"

"I beg your..." Vulcan stopped himself.

"You do realize all your work is for nothing now, don't you?"

The other four members of the Phoenix Force moved in as if to underscore his meaning.

"I don't know what you're talking about," Vulcan said huffily, and took his companion's arm.

Katz didn't let him leave.

"Come on, Vulcan. It's over. We get the whole picture: the training town, the planting of agents throughout the States, and now this, your grand finale."

Vulcan appealed to the other four men as if he were appealing to sanity in the face of a madman. "Is this gentlemen a friend of yours?"

They answered "Yes," in unison.

"Has he been drinking?"

"Forget the bullshit," McCarter said. "The game is over."

"Game? I have no idea what you are talking about," Vulcan persisted.

Gary Manning threw in a new idea. "Why don't you defect to the States? Tell your story and live a life of luxury."

"Defect? What do you mean? I'm an American citizen. I was born there. So was Miss Cardwell."

"Really—" Ann made a motion with her shoulders to show impatience and disgust "—this is getting ridiculous. I think you're all drunk. Come, Arnold. Let's go to the chapel."

"Yes, excuse us, gentlemen," Vulcan said. "We hold a midnight service for Christians aboard." He smiled. "Well, it's rather well past midnight. We cannot compete with the midnight buffet."

"We'll pray for your friend," Ann Cardwell said to the others, referring to Katz.

"Yes," Vulcan said. "Alcoholism is an illness that God's grace can cure."

They took the companionway leading down, leaving the five men with disbelieving expressions on their faces.

"I don't believe it," Katz said.

"Believe what?" James asked.

"Those two. We burned more than half their town, left enough bodies that they'll need a new cemetery, and not an hour ago I killed two of the gangsters they left behind to finish me. Now they pretend they don't know me. That's insane. They must know their cover is blown."

"You sure they're the right people?" Encizo questioned.

"'Sure'?" Katz repeated, and his chilly eyes showed his fury.

"Don't get excited," Calvin James intervened. "We didn't see anybody in Cheyenne that we didn't kill."

"You saw them," Katz told Manning and McCarter.

"The woman," Manning said. "For a second after we had nabbed the busboy."

"Then you, David?"

"Saw her between winks, yes."

"Are you saying I'm the only one who is certain about these people?" Katz was angry.

"Cool down, chief," Manning said.

"No wonder they think they can bluff their way out of their predicament. I'm the only one who's certain. It wouldn't stand up in court."

McCarter laughed derisively. "Since when do we settle things in court? You saw him. Then it's over. I wouldn't give a tinker's dam for their chances of getting to the States alive."

"Maybe they know something you don't," James suggested.

"Like what?"

"I don't know."

They were alone in the elevator, headed toward the upper deck, the most desirable location on board, where their adjoining suites were located.

"You killed two of Vulcan's men? That is the name he's using aboard the ship, by the way," Calvin James said. "And she's going by the name of Ann Cardwell all right."

"But what about the blokes you killed?" McCarter asked.

Katz was brief. "I tailed a bus when I saw the Cardwell woman go aboard. Like I said, I remembered her from Cheyenne."

"And..."

"I tagged along. Dull at first. In and out of mosques and churches all afternoon. We ended up at a restaurant for dinner. The woman lured me outside onto a narrow balcony, probably ten stories high. She left me out there with two airhead bully boys from her table. It was a toss-up. They lost, but they beat me down to street level by five minutes at least. And now she thinks she can bluff. It's beyond me."

They left the elevator and started down the deserted hallways toward Katz's suite—they shared two others between them—and once they were inside, knowing the place had checked out earlier and was secure from listening devices, started the briefing session.

"Have you talked to Brognola since your first phone call?" Gary Manning.

"No." Katz stopped consideringly, then continued. "I couldn't talk openly to Hal over the phone. But, given the clues I dropped, I'm sure he gets the picture: Cheyenne, a KGB training emplacement. Burned...he would know that from spy satellites." They all exchanged a look, as if following one another's thoughts. "He knows we're aboard the *Odyssey*, and I'm sure he got the message that we were trailing people from Russia's Cheyenne. And he'll know we'll be reaching Venice just shortly before the President speaks to all of these computer brains."

"It doesn't sound like you need contact him again soon," McCarter said.

Manning agreed. "Vulcan and his gang have us pegged. Any communication with Stony Man can endanger the overall operation. We have to be supercareful."

"Agreed," Encizo and James said, then started moving restlessly about the room.

After a short planning session, Katz began handing out assignments.

"All right, McCarter, how about getting us a passenger list?"

"There's one in every room."

"Okay, check for newcomers besides us. Get the list to Hal. Maybe he can make use of the names and addresses."

"Send it in the clear?"

"Why not? Everybody knows their own name. As long as it doesn't go straight to headquarters."

"What about me?" Calvin asked.

"Tail Vulcan. Forget everything else."

"You going after the Cardwell woman yourself?" McCarter asked.

Katz looked somewhat regretful and grim. "Yes." Sighing with weariness, he leaned back on the couch, knowing he would have to shower before he could sleep. Encizo brought some coffee over from the bar, and the Israeli accepted a cup gratefully.

"I still don't know how Vulcan and his gang hope to survive when we know all about them."

Manning replied in an emotionless voice, "They kill all of us. That's how."

"The man has a point," James admitted.

Katz nodded. "Yes, we'll do well to keep that in mind."

"Maybe they intend to disembark in Mykanos," Encizo said.

Katz nodded. "Good point. Check with the purser to see if anyone is scheduled to leave the ship at the island. I doubt that there will be. But if Vulcan, Cardwell, or any of their bunch doesn't return to the ship, we notify the local authorities."

"Mykanos?" Gary Manning said. "The Greek government doesn't cooperate with the U.S. much any more. They've got a socialist government who thinks we side with their old enemies the Turks."

"Then we make sure they all get back aboard after touring the island. We disable anyone who we suspect of trying to escape."

"And in Venice?" McCarter asked.

Katz closed his eyes. "Before we get there, I'll have instructions from Brognola."

He was tired, but he stayed awake to question the four warriors. "Did any of you get something worthwhile from your surveillance today?"

McCarter shook his head.

"Nada," Encizo said.

Manning agreed. "A waste of time."

"You had the Russian's bus to tail," Calvin James said. "I just got suntanned."

"Don't fall into that way of thinking. Undoubtedly not all of the Russians rode around together." Katz checked his watch. "Everything's closed aboard ship except the disco, so turn in early or see what you can find to amuse yourselves. And be careful. Carry arms. These people may look like nice down-home folks from Cheyenne, but as they showed us, they're all trained killers."

He stood in the doorway after the others had gone, feeling somewhat let down as he started to close the door behind him.

"Wait," someone called to him from the corridor, and he whirled around to see the Cardwell woman at the end of the short hallway.

"You killed those two men, didn't you?" she asked matter-of-factly.

He was startled to see her, but he tried to hide his shock. "*You* killed them," Katz replied. "You sent them out onto the balcony."

He felt strangely uneasy. The woman was, he knew without a doubt, a dangerous seductress, besides being a KGB agent. She had lured him onto the balcony and tried to have him killed. Yet he was drawn to her with the kind of attraction he had felt when he had first met his wife. But he was widowed, and that kind of closeness was long gone. There were women, attractive, too, but without the kind of pull he was experiencing with the Russian woman.

"They only meant to talk with you," she said.

He laughed.

"Sure."

"You murdered them like all those innocent people back at Cheyenne. If Moscow ties you to that slaughter, your own government would arrest all of you."

Katz had heard the same thought expressed a dozen times during his tenure on Phoenix Force.

"It won't wash, Ann, or whatever your real name is. Once you're inside the States, you can use the American laws, the Constitution, the entire judicial system, to get away with whatever nefarious scheme you've got concocted. But out here, I'm judge, jury..."

"And executioner."

"Yes, that, too. It's not a job I like. But somebody has to work around the laws..."

"Outside the laws," she said. "You're an outlaw."

He nodded. "Yes. Occasionally I am an outlaw."

"You're breaking the laws of the freest nation in the world. You're defying the Constitution with the most magnificent bill of human rights written since the beginning of civilization. People all over the world dream of going to the United States, not because they have more fast-food restaurants or better housing than virtually anyone else. It's the legal systems, the freedoms that beckon so many of us. I mean—"

Katz walked toward her as he understood what she meant.

"You're doing this because you want to defect to America?"

"No."

"Yes." He was only a half dozen steps away from her, alert for the slightest movement on her part. Deliberately he pretended to be careless. He did not look back over his shoulder but could check her movements in a mirroring effect from the brass wall-hanging that depicted an artist's conception of a ship. "How many of your Cheyenne graduates have the same idea?''

''None,'' she said.

''Afraid Vulcan will hear you admit what you have planned?''

''No. I have no secrets from him.''

He came so close that he could enjoy her perfume. Then, unable to resist, and swayed by her heady scent to disregard what was a mild sense of danger, he put his finger under her her chin, tilting her head toward him, and kissed her gently. She neither resisted nor welcomed him with her lips.

He drew back to look at her again.

''You know one of us will get off this ship in a body bag,'' he said.

''I know. I wish it weren't so.''

She turned and walked away.

And he felt sad. He knew how lonely the lovely suite would be.

Inside, he searched the lavishly furnished quarters, which included a sliding glass door to a small outside terrace on a balcony hanging out over the sea. That was the weakest point in his defenses. He pulled the drapes, planning to sleep there on the floor.

The clothes from one unlocked suitcase had been unpacked and put away, but his attaché case sat where he had left it. He opened it after checking for a booby trap and extracted the Titan Tiger .38 Special he had bought in Turkey. A good dependable defender, it would not have been his first choice. In the Turkish bazaar, though, variety had been limited. And the two-inch barrel fit well in his waistband. A sweater covered it easily.

He dropped to the couch. He had exhausted himself and considered sleeping fully clothed, but duty interfered. He had an idea.

He picked up the telephone and dialed the radio room's number. He had thought of a way to alert Hal Brognola without jeopardizing the headquarters' security.

The ringing in his ear jarred him enough to keep him awake.

No one answered in the radio room, and he dialed the purser's desk.

A female's bright voice greeted him.

"Is the radio room open?" he asked.

"It is always open," the girl answered pertly. "But normally they do not place passengers' calls until nine in the morning."

"Unless it's an emergency?"

"Yes. I am certain they would put through an emergency call at anytime. Do you want me to ring them for you?"

"No. I called. No one answered."

"That is strange."

"I'll go up. The man on duty might have fallen asleep."

"Heavens. I hope not. Let me know what you find."

"Certainly."

After hanging up, he looked at the ship's sales brochure on the suite's large walnut desk. The crosscut map of the ship showed he was only one deck down from the radio room.

He left the room cautiously and climbed the companionway. At the radio room, the window was closed. He rapped repeatedly with his knuckles. No answer.

The door's metal knob offered no resistance, and it turned easily, letting the door swing back into the fully lit room.

Cabinets of radio gear closed off one wall. The desk, chair, and short stand-up microphone were neatly placed. Everything was shipshape except two drawers of radio gear that were not fitted tightly into their cabinets.

Katz pulled them out.

Slots for circuit boards were empty. Loose connections hung free like guts from a fish partly cleaned.

The computer and its modem appeared untouched, until Katz lifted the monitor and fan device and looked in. There was not a single board inside. Granted that the ports might have been enough for most programs and communications, the fan was a giveaway. The computer was self-cooling unless the inside was packed with extra cards.

No doubt about it.

The communications equipment had been vandalized.

Katz then confirmed it for himself. He could not even get static in the headset or a flicker on the monitor.

His concern increased as he found more cabinets on the other side of the room. The cabinets were bare. They must have been stripped of replacement parts.

With deliberate calm, he dialed the bridge and asked for the duty officer.

"I want to place a call to the States," he said.

"Too late." The duty officer's voice was heavy with a Scandinavian accent.

"This is an emergency," Katz added.

"Then call the radio room, please. The operator will help you, I am certain."

"I did call. There was no answer."

"Impossible. You dialed the wrong number."

"No. I'm in the radio room. There is no one on duty."

"Wait then. The operator must have stepped out."

"Permanently, I'm afraid."

"Permanently? What is this?"

"I think you are going to find you have no radio communications and no spare parts."

"Impossible."

"Tell me that after you have checked the communications systems."

"I will be down. Wait for me there."

"Sure," Katz said as he hung up the phone and left the small quarters. He paused on the companionway leading to his deck until he heard the exclamations of the ship's officers as they entered the vandalized shack.

No radio, he told himself. Interesting.

No doubt Vulcan's people had started work on their plan. Stopping them, whatever their goal, was his job. And it was bound to be a nasty one.

18

They gathered in Katz's suite, out on the terrace where the dense fog cloaked their muted vision in cotton. The remains of hearty lunches lay before them. A mixture of dishes spoke of their different backgrounds. Each dish identified the man: bagels for Katz, mackerel for Encizo, Canadian bacon for Manning, mixed grill for McCarter, and grits for Calvin James. But actually their selection was made more as a test of the ship's larder than any particular taste for the respective ethnic dishes.

The cuisine confirmed the reputation of cruise ships. There was food for every taste from caviar to chicken-fried steak with mashed potatoes and gravy.

Another element had influenced the men's choice of food. In twelve hours they had learned one thing: they were in a self-enclosed environment, outnumbered by a largely unknown enemy. But the enemy would have no trouble getting to know the five of them.

"Great last meal," Calvin James said with an irony they could appreciate, except for McCarter, who glared threateningly at the young black, then sipped at a cup of hot tea.

Manning finished his third Coca-Cola of the day. The others opted for coffee.

"All right, where do we stand?" Katz's words rapped like a judge's gavel. "Let's get a good situation report."

Encizo spoke gloomily. "Up that proverbial creek with toothpicks for paddles."

Gary Manning stood up, knocking over his Coke and letting it flow across the embroidered tablecloth.

"Cut out the damned gallows humor," he grumbled. "I'm no more afraid of dying than either of you, but I don't want to go out a loser."

"I say it again," McCarter entered the conversation belligerently. "We get their leaders—the Cardwell woman and Vulcan—and the whole plot folds for lack of leadership."

"No," Katz said quietly but sharply. "I told you that it's too late for that. The plan is set. It goes off on schedule whether they're dead or not."

"Why do you still think it's the right thing?"

"He told you," James intervened. "We've watched them up until thirty minutes ago. They're holed up in his room. They haven't let anybody in and haven't used the phone. They're waiting for—"

"I could almost swear you're jealous, Katz," McCarter, not known for his tact, remarked rudely, more as a way of releasing tension than out of malice. "The two of them spending the night together, and now all morning, too."

"I find her an attractive woman, but this is a very important mission, and my personal longings do not enter it. Aside from that, though, she has a magnetic force. I am all too familiar with her type."

None of them spoke, and a sympathetic silence descended. They had all experienced what it was like to feel for somebody who was by all appearances undeserving.

McCarter, who'd expected Katz to fight back, hung his head with remorse. It was the helplessness of feeling trapped that had gotten to him, he decided. Why, he admired Katz more than anybody else.

"Sorry," he said. He rarely apologized. This time it made him feel better.

Katz nodded. "Forget it. So let's get on with that situation report. I'll start things moving."

"One radio man is missing. The equipment and spares have been knowledgeably sabotaged."

With the tension gone, the men became professionals again.

"The captain says the system is shut down temporarily for routine maintenance," Encizo said. "That's what I was told when I tried to put through a call first thing this morning like you told me to do."

Katz laughed cynically. "No skipper shuts down his links to the outside world when he has a thousand passengers aboard."

"The radar is on the fritz," Manning reported. "The sonar can't hear a thing, and the foghorn has laryngitis. They have signal flags up, visible about ten yards off either side."

Calvin James contributed. "They're firing the Very pistol, but nobody with radar is going to pass close enough to see them."

"And from what I gather," Manning said, "I'd bet a bearskin rug against a skunk hat that all the navigational equipment is spinning around like ballerinas. This ship is in the ocean of piss as far as I can tell."

"So," Katz said. "We're cut off from the world. Absolutely cut off."

"Too many coincidences," McCarter added. "Everything except the fog could be sabotage."

Katz nodded his head. "So we work on that presumption. The Cheyenne gang has cut us off from civilization and forced the skipper to proceed at steerage speed. And we only know two people from the other side."

"Except there is no Cheyenne gang," Encizo said.

"What do you mean?"

"I had to sweet-talk an ugly *muchacha* from the purser's office most of the night. She tells me there are only two people aboard from Cheyenne: Cardwell and Vulcan."

"You saw the passports?"

"No. She told me. If you want me to..."

"Never mind," McCarter said. "You're right."

"How do you know?"

"Elementary, my dear Watson." He tossed a copy of the passenger list on the table. "It includes hometowns. The church bus you followed, Katz, the group that nearly got you killed might have had less than half a dozen of the Cheyenne people along. We can be sure of no one except Cardwell, Vulcan and the two goons."

Katz said, "So there is only one large identifiable group aboard the ship. The computer experts."

"And they're clean," Manning said. "They're all well-known. To the industry. To the government. And each other. There are no Cheyenne people in that group. I guarantee it."

Katz sorted through his memory. "I thought we had this game going into the last quarter with a twenty-one point lead. Now it seems we have nothing."

"We have Cardwell and Vulcan. We could sweat them," McCarter said. His friends' eyes were unenthusiastic when they looked at him. "Yeah, yeah, they'd lie. But maybe their cohorts in this thing would come out in the open to help them."

Manning interrupted. "That's why they're holed up. You try to go into that stateroom, and I guarantee you'll go off this ship as chum for the local fisherman."

"Blast!" McCarter stared at the floor.

"By tomorrow morning, the shipping company will begin an air-sea search for the *Odyssey*," Encizo said.

"Where did you hear that?" Katz asked.

"I heard the cabin stewards talking."

Manning scoffed. "That's getting the news from the horse's ass."

"No, wait," Katz said. "They're undoubtedly right. They will start a search, and they'll find us fast."

"So we turn Cardwell and Vulcan in to the authorities. Let the CIA sort out the agents."

Katz smacked the metal of his artificial hand into his remaining palm. "You don't understand. Whatever they're up to, the Cheyenne troops are going to pull it off by tomorrow morning."

"Like what?" Encizo asked.

McCarter volunteered an idea. "Like getting off the ship in lifeboats and heading for a Greek island. Around here islands are as thick as dung in a pasture."

"That means they won't get a chance to assassinate or kidnap the President in Venice, Katz," Calvin James said.

"If they're going to escape by lifeboat, what are they waiting for? The fog isn't going to last. The captain can navigate with a sextant," Katz spit out as he paced the floor.

"Then we've beaten them," McCarter said. "They'll never get through Greek paperwork in time to reach Venice. I mean, they show up on shore in lifeboats from a ship that hasn't sunk. They're going nowhere. Call them, Katz. Tell Vulcan we'll let them go without a fight." Impetuously he looked in the ship's phone directory and dialed Vulcan's phone number. He handed the instrument to Katz.

After a brief greeting, Katz went to the point. "Got an offer for you, 'Reverend.' If you and all...I emphasize all...if you want to get off the ship in lifeboats..."

"Lifeboats? Leave the ship?" The Russian sounded incredulous. "Good heavens. We certainly have no intentions of deserting a perfectly good ship. You really must see someone about your drinking, Mr....Mr...."

"Dwayne Fredericks," Katz lied.

"Yes, well, Mr. Fredericks, please do not call again. Miss Cardwell and I are preparing my weekly sermon."

The phone clicked and Katz shook his head.

When he put it aside, no one doubted the response.

But Calvin James approached things from a different viewpoint. "Maybe we're missing the point." He furrowed his brow and felt ill at ease making a suggestion to men far more experienced than himself. But a pebble of thought was in his brain, and he could not cover it over the way an oyster makes a pearl. "Maybe the Russian mission does not require them to reach the States. Maybe they don't even have to reach Venice. I mean...getting a bunch of agents into the States at one time might be a big bonus. And killing or kidnapping the President by agents pretending to be American citizens might have some advantage. But what if their mission is right here."

Manning smirked. "Aboard ship?"

"Yeah."

"Like doing what?"

James began retreating. "It was just a thought."

"They could break up the shuffleboard tournament," McCarter said.

James tried to salvage something of his idea. "Maybe they know we are Phoenix Force agents. We may be the only target."

"They didn't know we'd come aboard," Katz argued.

"Or they could plan on sinking the ship? To kill a lot of people."

Katz again disregarded the idea. "The last time a cruise ship sank, three people were injured when they were getting into the lifeboats. And that was off Alaska."

Katz rubbed the bridge of his nose the way people did who wore glasses constantly. Something was definitely starting to nag at him.

"Katz—" Gary Manning caught the Phoenix Force leader's attention and nodded toward the door leading to the hall.

A slip of paper slid through the crack beneath.

Five hands reached for concealed weapons, but only McCarter actually drew his piece.

"I'll get it." Encizo put a detaining hand on his leader's shoulder and then crossed the living room. He returned with the folded paper unopened.

Katz read it twice to himself before reading it aloud. "Captain Nielson invites you and your traveling companions to join the assistant cruise director on an exclusive tour of the *Odyssey*'s engine room, promptly at 5:00 p.m. today."

He raised his eyes and looked from one man to another.

Manning reacted first. He took the note from Katz and said, "It's typed."

"So it's not a regular invitation," Encizo said.

Katz took it back. "Few cruise ships let their passengers into the engine rooms. They cite insurance rules. You get guided tours of the bridge, and sometimes they show off their kitchens...but engine rooms? Not usually."

"Then you're sure this came from Vulcan?" Manning asked.

"Anyone doubt it?"

"No," McCarter said.

James shrugged.

"Not me," said Encizo. "But why 5:00 p.m.?"

"It's after tea time," McCarter said. "Just before bingo. A quarter of the passengers will be in the main lounge with their little cards."

"What about the rest?"

McCarter cocked his head. "The pianist will be playing classical music in a cozy bar. Bridge in the card room. A few of the ladies will be finishing up in the hairdresser's. And cocktails will be served at every bar aboard."

"And the crew?" Katz asked.

"Between bells? The captain and half his officers will be dressing for dinner. Can't let the fat cats dine without giving proper importance to the occasion, you know." McCarter smiled. "That should include us before the cruise is over. We have the most expensive suites. That's usually the ticket to the captain's table or at least the honor of having the ship's engineer at your table. The kitchen help will be busy as hell, of course. The waiters and busboys will be setting the tables. Half the crew will have eaten earlier. The other half will be dining belowdecks. Cruise director and staff, let's see... anyone not at bingo will be at the singles' party. The disco chap will still be sleeping. The entertainers... getting into costume, I imagine."

"What about the theater?" Katz asked.

"The cinema?"

"Yes."

"Showing the end of a film, probably."

"And the grand master computer hackers of the Western world will be at their machines."

"Wrong on both of those notions." Manning had picked up the daily bulletin of ship's entertainment. "No matinee movie today. The master hackers have a seminar in the movie theater between four and six. So any kiddies aboard will be at the pool, gawking at the girls in G-strings."

Katz nodded. "In other words, practically everybody aboard will be busy?"

"Ho! I do believe you have it. The invitation gets you into the engine room while everybody else is otherwise occupied. Clever chaps, these Russian cowboys from Cheyenne."

"Only one error in your thinking, McCarter," Manning said. "One, we'll all be in that engine room. They'll have more to contend with than they expect."

Katz said, "Only three problems with your thinking, Gary. Vulcan knows damn well I'll expect a trap. Two, he'll know all of you will be there to back me up. And three, they know what to expect from us, and they're not the least bit afraid."

"Meaning?"

"I don't know. But five o'clock is like high noon."

"Cheyenne showdown," Calvin James.

"Yes," Katz agreed. "Cheyenne showdown at 5:00 p.m."

19

The Phoenix Force team had scouted the engine room entrances, three hours before the "deadline" that had been specified on the odd invitation.

Restrictive signs like Crew Only had meant nothing. With five hundred employees, nobody knew all of them. A staff, trained in how to cater to passengers, found it difficult to deny access to any part of the ship to the paying guests.

Not wanting to call attention to themselves, only one of the Force, Rafael Encizo, had actually entered the engine room.

Back in Katz's suite, he drew a map of the lower two decks of the ship.

The others grouped around the table to hear him out. They had spent their afternoon playing detective, trying to pin down who worked with Vulcan. It was boring work for active men.

Without enjoyment Katz dragged on another Camel: his mouth tasted bad, and finally he determinedly squashed the unfinished cigarette. Butts filled the ashtrays to overflowing. Manning drank Coca-Cola. Empty and partially filled cans around the room spoke of his tension—and his addiction.

McCarter played with the gun he intended to carry in the holster covered by his turtleneck sweater. For the fourth time he emptied the magazine of the M-S Safari Arms Matchmaster .45-caliber pistol and recounted the shells. The seven-shot magazine was not enough, considering that he had no reserve whatsoever.

He scowled each time he refilled the clip.

Finishing touches and details on the sketch of the deck plans occupied Encizo, who was usually calm but appeared somewhat high-strung.

Only Calvin James watched patiently, and even he was obsessed with the digital wall clock, checking it every twenty to thirty seconds.

Twenty minutes, thirty-two seconds before the deadline. Twenty minutes, twelve seconds before 5:00 p.m.

"Okay." Katz exhaled two lungsful of smoke to cloud the table the way fog had restricted the ship captain's vision throughout the day. "Go through it slowly, Rafael."

"All right. Near as I can tell, beneath the bottom deck there's a sort of crawl space."

"The bilges," McCarter offered.

"Yeah," Encizo said. "You could reach it from the engine room. There's a hatch in the deck, but it looks as if the locking mechanism has been painted over. So let's skip that and go straight to the bottom deck and the engine room itself.

"The front half of the bottom deck is filled with storage and fuel tanks. There is a hatch between the storage compartment and the engine room. We could enter from there, except we'd have to get inside the storage area. That would involve breaking a sturdy lock on a companionway from above, or using a locked freight elevator. I'd call that approach possible but not plausible."

Manning snorted, but never voiced what his problem was. With a baleful eye he looked at McCarter when he spoke.

"Leaving us what?" McCarter asked impatiently.

Katz said, "Let him tell it, David. We still have eighteen minutes left."

Seventeen minutes, forty-six seconds, James told himself.

The Cuban continued, carefully choosing his words. "The engine room occupies the stern half of the bottom deck. Just what you would expect. Three giant diesels. Generators. A complete tool shop. Lathes, drill presses, that sort of thing."

"Just tell us how you got in," Calvin James interrupted. He could not keep his eyes from locking on the clock.

"All right. The engine room occupies the entire back half of the bottom deck. On the starboard side, though, it's two decks high. I guess they needed the extra space for piping, wiring, catwalks out over the engines. That means the main entrance to the engine room is from the second deck up.

"Crew quarters all the way to the bow. At the stern is the auditorium. It must seat half the passengers aboard and also serves as the movie theater.

"And that's the way we go into the engine room," Encizo decided.

"You running the team now, Encizo?" McCarter asked snidely.

Katz ignored the Englishman. "What makes that the best way in?"

"First, that route gets us to the second deck up without attracting any attention. Anybody asks... which is unlikely...we say we're going to the movie."

"Better say we're looking for the computer seminar. The bits and bytes people will be occupying the auditorium then," Katz said.

"Okay." Encizo continued. "The door to the hallway leading forward has a small sign that reads Crew's Quarters. There's no big Passengers Forbidden sign. We won't get thrown out before we reach the engine room door."

"What makes you sure," McCarter said caustically this time, but nobody bothered responding to that.

"You can babble in Russian and French, Katz, if anybody tries to stop us." The suggestion was Calvin James's. "Rafael can spiel out in Spanish. You do your Cockney imitation, David."

McCarter grunted.

"Of course the Russians will expect us to enter through that door," Katz said.

Encizo nodded. "No question about it. When you go through that door, you're a sitting duck. You can take the stairway down or walk out onto the catwalks. Take your choice."

McCarter grumbled. "All they have to do is pick us off one at a time as we come through the door."

Manning took a swig of Coke and shook his head. "We can all get in there alive."

"How?" McCarter asked.

"They'll want Katz for sure."

"So?"

"So he goes in last."

"What?" McCarter was incredulous.

Calvin James understood. "Sure. I'll go in first. They won't mistake me for Katz."

Encizo said, "Me next."

Manning shrugged. "Sounds good. If they kill three of us, they can't expect Katz will ever come through that door."

"Throw in smoke," McCarter said. "We got the stuff. Stun bombs. I have several I bought at the bazaar in Istanbul."

"Better throw in everything first, before any of you go in," Katz suggested.

"No." Calvin James was emphatic. "Sorry, Katz. I didn't mean to take over."

"No problem. Go ahead."

"I just think I should carry a stun grenade, Rafael, the smoke, but I don't see using it until we know where the guys are who are attempting to ambush us. I'm sure they won't shoot anybody if it means losing a chance at Katz. The rest of us are small-fry to the Cheyenne bunch."

Katz looked from one to the other. "Well. Gary?"

"It sure isn't SWAT team tactics, but under the circumstances, it sounds good."

"Rafael?"

"It makes sense."

"Calvin, we know what you think. How about you, David?"

McCarter paused. "Yeah, yeah. I like it. But what about afterward?"

All eyes focused on Katz, but it was Calvin James, the Seals-trained frogman, who answered.

"If it becomes necessary for us to abandon ship, then here is the escape plan. Because I doubt you guys can swim as far as me, so in five minutes...no more... after the shooting is over, or the last bad guy is down, we meet on Promenade Deck, forward. I'll have a lifeboat ready to launch."

"He waits for nobody," Katz said. "Not me. Not any of you. One of us has to get word back to Stony Man. If you're late, get your own lifeboat."

The others said nothing until Katz looked at the clock.

Before he could read it, Calvin James interpreted for him.

"We have two minutes, Katz, if we want to be on time."

"We do."

Katz stood up, and then they were all standing, exchanging a long look of trust and confidence that they would each do their best.

"Okay, we meet outside the theater. Everybody takes a different route as far as possible."

A final nervousness before going into action made McCarter launch a last unhelpful comment. "We're walking into a trap," he said, "and we know it."

Katz shifted the pistol in his belt. "You know David, if you knew there was a tiger lurking at a water hole, threatening everybody, you'd head straight there and kill the SOB."

McCarter grunted, and was the first to start out.

Two minutes later they converged in the stairwell outside the ship's auditorium. Through the lustrous wooden doors they heard a heated debate on quantum jumps in voice-operated computers.

McCarter stood at the top of the stairs, making certain they would not be trapped even before they reached the engine room, and he continued to bring up the rear as the team moved cautiously through the crew's quarters. There, luxury ended. The air-conditioning failed.

The open doors afforded views of men sitting idly on the edges of their bunks. On upper bunks men stared at the ceiling.

Crew members crowded the corridor. A few stood around smoking. Others carried paint and brushes as they moved out on some job or other. A number of them were equipped with mops and brooms. The sound of a harmonica drifted from one of the dreary rooms. A man trotted by with a ladder, while another hurried somewhere with a tool key.

A quarter of the way toward the bow, they encountered the first detail that Encizo had left out. There was a steel door that led off the main corridor. The Cuban swung it open.

"Hey—" Katz caught Rafael's arm "—you didn't say anything about this."

Encizo appeared hurt. He apologized and said, "It's nothing. It's okay."

But it was not okay to Katz. The corridor was short, a dead end, and poorly lit.

"David," Katz said.

Calling his name was enough. McCarter knew what to do. He stayed in the main hallway while the others proceeded.

Inside the branch hall, Katz kept his left hand close to his gun.

A swarthy man was just opening the only door off the hall as Phoenix Force approached.

The man grinned.

For a moment Katz thought the man was acting as doorman for the Phoenix bunch, then relaxed somewhat as two other crewmen rolled a heavy welding rig with two big cylinders from inside the engine room.

They were obviously headed somewhere aboard the ship for a repair job.

James and Encizo had already entered the engine room, Calvin taking the stairs and Rafael walking out across the catwalks.

Manning gave an all-clear signal.

A moment later McCarter and Katz were both inside and found the noise level painful. The engines worked at a pace that sounded like panic. The shafts to the propellers were enclosed, but the screws fought the sea like giant marlin at the end of a hook. There were other unidentifiable sounds: clicks, tappings, hissing. Had the room been dark, it would have been frightening.

But it was well lit, showing off banks of gauges and endless strands of cabling and a network of hoses and pipes. All cream white, the room was meticulously clean.

In the enormous room, Katz watched while his men searched for hiding places, of which there were many. The doors to the forward storage compartment had to be guarded, and the tool room needed thorough checking, besides.

There was a roaring air conditioner working somewhere in the enormous two-deck high room, but the humidity hung like fog. Perspiration coursed down Katz's back. It ran from his forehead into his eyes. He had to take his hand from his weapon in order to clear his sight.

They had been searching for more than five minutes before any of them became restless enough to look toward Katz.

He was scowling.

He had expected Vulcan or his men to be waiting.

"Manning. McCarter," he shouted. "Open that door."

With the engines pounding and peripherals wheezing, there was no hearing inside the giant engine room unless men stood close to one another, cupped their hands and shouted directly into the ear.

Katz changed to sign language. The two men understood. One took good cover while the other went to open the door.

Nothing happened.

The handle and unlocking devices worked, but the door didn't budge.

"James, Encizo." Katz motioned them to the other door. The results were the same.

He sensed a trick. In a second either or both of the doors would open, and Cheyenne killers could come streaming in.

McCarter and Encizo knew the countermove. They sought cover, aimed weapons at the door, and held stun grenades in preparation.

Nothing happened.

Katz moved partway down the stairs, half of his attention fixed on the door through which they had entered.

Manning and James took up the search again.

Finally, James stopped and went down on his knees. He holstered his gun and probed under one of the big fuel tanks. When he withdrew his hands, they were smeared with blood.

Katz immediately sensed they had been outfoxed. He didn't know how yet, but he felt the warning signals in his body. His hard stomach tightened. His eyes darted over to the entrance. He became all too aware that there was no engine room crewman in sight. While good maintenance could keep the enormous diesels working around the clock for weeks at a time, they would never be left untended for a minute.

Calvin was drawing a bloody body from beneath the tanks.

It was dressed in the dark brown khaki that many men wore on such jobs. Then James brought out a second body.

When the handsome black man looked up for orders, Katz motioned him toward the small office near the front. He pretended he was holding a telephone receiver to his ear.

James came out carrying the phone and dragging the cut line.

Katz was not surprised. It had dawned on him that the lone crewman who had held the door for them earlier had not entered with them but had hurried back up the stairs.

He tried the handle. It moved reassuringly in his hand.

The relief lasted only until he tried to open the hatch. It refused to budge. He rapped on it with his pistol. No answer. He put his ear close to the door and jerked away immediately. The door's surface had felt quite hot.

James came running up the steps.

"There's a third and maybe a fourth body under there," he said. "What's wrong here?"

"They've welded the door shut."

"Huh?"

"You heard me."

The black Yank gaped. He had been hit, shot at, tripped, cut, pummeled, kicked, but never before had he fallen victim to a welder's torch.

Katz leaned over the railing and signaled to Encizo and McCarter. They understood and worked harder to attempt to force open the doors they had been guarding. There was no response. Both men were still trying to figure out what they were doing wrong when Katz waved them off.

"No use." He tried to form the words clearly enough for his lips to be read.

Coming down the ladder, he motioned all of them to join him in the small office. Only Manning dallied. He took his time poking into nooks and crannies, and when he did come in he was carrying a shoebox.

"We're locked in," Katz started to explain immediately. "Those two with the acetylene torch must have done it the moment we stepped inside."

"The same thing over at our doors," McCarter said. "Only they did the job from the inside. You can see the weld. We'd need something powerful to break it."

"And the phone line to the bridge is cut," James said. "I gather we're cut off completely."

"Maybe there's another torch," McCarter told Katz.

"We'll look," he said, "but I doubt they're that stupid."

"We can hammer on the doors until someone hears us," Encizo suggested. Then he had a better idea. "We could stop the engines. That would get attention from the bridge quickly."

"We may be giving away our cover," Katz suggested.

"We're locked in here with three corpses," Manning said. "I think we'd be useless to Phoenix Force if we're caught with them."

"We're up against some clever people," Katz said. "They'll be abandoning ship soon."

"Everybody will be," Manning said. "Except for us, at least."

The four others turned to stare at him.

"What are you talking about?" McCarter asked.

"This."

He opened the shoe box. It held a solid block of brownish material taped to a pair of batteries, a watch and the cap from a shotgun shell.

"For God's sake!" Katz exclaimed. "Defuse that thing."

"Can't do it."

"But you're the expert on defusing plastique."

"With tools, with time. Knowing how to defuse a bomb takes training. Knowing you can't do it in time makes you an expert. A living expert. And I can't stop this baby from blowing. Besides..."

"Yes, hurry, tell us," Katz prompted.

"There's at least one other bomb planted down here."

The other four waited.

"It's tucked far down the propeller shaft. I can see it, but I haven't a prayer of bringing it back up in time."

"Are you sure they managed to get it down there?" Encizo griped.

"Yes, and they had more than five minutes to get it into place."

They took an involuntary step back.

Katz spoke for the group. "You saying that thing in your hand is going to blow in five minutes?"

"Four minutes, thirty-two seconds to be precise. Four, thirty-one now. Thirty seconds, et cetera, et cetera."

"Heave it," James shouted.

"Get behind something," Katz said coolly.

"I can heave it, of course, and we can hide behind the engines and come out of this with nothing worse than a broken eardrum or two."

"Then heave it."

McCarter and James were backing out from the office, and Katz and Encizo followed.

So did Manning. Unlike the others, he was curious about the device, turning it over and over in his hand as the seconds continued to click off this watch.

"The problem, gentlemen, is this. As I said, there is another device down the propeller shaft, and I suspect there may be more in here and perhaps down in the bilges. In any case, one of those others is going to blow a hole in the hull of this ship. Below the water line. In other words, the ship is going to sink, and we're going to be among the first to drown."

20

"Blast our way out," Katz told Manning. "Blow the door off."

"I hope I can," Gary said. "This timer on the outside looks like a high school kid put it together. I wouldn't be surprised to find a real detonator that works another way. But there's no time to find out. The rest of you take cover."

Katz motioned, and the team scampered for cover as Manning carried the bomb up the stairs. He fixed it against the door and rushed downstairs to join Katz in the office.

"You know," he said, thinking aloud, "Vulcan left that device where we'd find it so we could blast a way out after they welded us in."

"That doesn't make much sense," Katz stated.

"Unless," Gary continued, "that bomb won't go off until the water has filled the room."

Katz stared at Manning, his mind swimming with plots and counterplots that might have gone through Arnold Vulcan's mind. "You're saying they wanted us dead, but they wanted it to look like we sank the ship." Katz worked that around in his head.

"Precisely. They wanted the engine room crew dead. They wanted the doors welded shut so no one could get at the bombs in time to defuse them."

Katz carried the thought further. "Then we dropped into the center of their plans. It was set to look as though we welded the doors shut..."

"So nobody could interfere while we were working. And finally, they provided us with a bomb to blow off one door so it would appear that we had an escape route planned."

"We're quite a serendipity for them," Katz thought aloud. "They sink the ship. We take the blame. That bastard Arnold Vulcan must be a real genius."

"Clever enough to build an entire town," Gary said.

Katz raised a hand. "But...wait...why do they want to sink the ship?"

"That I can't explain."

The engine room was suddenly transformed. There was a gargantuan roar that they heard despite the hands they had tightly clapped over their ears. A giant hole opened in the steel at the stern. Anything not fastened down hurled through a dark cloud of smoke streaked with lightning like spears of flame.

Three seconds later the ocean burst in as a funnel of water with a three-foot diameter smashed against the engines. Then it darted right through the tool room.

Electric lines sputtered. All but the overhead lights flicked out. Cabinets of gear tipped over and floated. The water became a whirlpool carrying debris and tossing the Phoenix Force men about.

When they could, they found a relatively quiet place behind the engines, which were rattling the loose propeller shafts apart.

McCarter growled at Manning. "I thought you were going to blow off the goddamned door."

"I thought I was. But the detonator on the outside is fake." He sounded as calm and pedantic as an aging professor of early European literature. "I suspect the bomb will go off a short time after it is immersed in water. Too late for us, unfortunately."

"Then go up there and throw a bucket of water on it," McCarter demanded.

"Thanks, but no."

They were treading water now and the ceiling seemed to be closing down upon them. James started to the ladder, ready to prolong his life to the last possible moment, but Manning shouted at him. "Stay away from there. You'll get in my way."

The engines sputtered and roared, then quit as Gary reached the stairway. At the top he faced his friends.

With the engines down, he could be heard.

"When I dive, you guys get under the water. Go as deep as you can and stay down as long as you can."

"What are you going to do?" Katz asked.

Manning cheerfully held up a stun grenade.

"Oh, shit," McCarter said. "That'll never dent that door."

"It will if it sets off the plastique."

Gary, using the wires from the phony detonator and shaping a place in the plastique, fit the grenade into the indentation. He took a floating cabinet and laid it against the door. Then he pulled the pin and held it up proudly before diving over the rail.

No one saw the explosion. They were underwater, holding their breath as long as they could. They came up, stroking toward the partially opened door. They tore at it until their hands bled. The twisted metal gave way slowly while the water began to lap at their ankles. Then there was room for Katz and Encizo to pass through. With an outside grip they managed to enlarge the hole enough for the other three.

A moment later they were free of the door. The ship's whistle sounded a terrifying cry.

The intercom came on. "All hands to your lifeboat stations. This is not a drill. Repeat, this is no drill. Prepare to close and latch all fireproof doors."

The corridor where the Phoenix Force team emerged was empty. Most of the crew stateroom doors stood open, revealing floors covered with clothes and other personal items. From above came the anguished cries of abject terror.

A list tilted the ship to starboard, and the bow was sinking faster than the stern. Vulcan had obviously placed bombs forward, too.

The inclined deck made running difficult. Katz, though, did not hesitate. As he moved awkwardly he stripped off his shirt and drew the Titan Tiger .38 Special he had bought in Istanbul.

He flung open the door that closed off the stairs and threw out his shirt.

A gun blasted. The shirt changed course.

Katz thrust out his Titan Tiger and fired. The slug tore into a surprised man, a soldier who served Vulcan, no doubt. He sat at the bottom of the companionway to the third deck. His hands covered his chest to staunch the flow of blood. Because the man's gun lay nearby, Katz shot him again to be certain.

Then he tried the auditorium door.

It had metamorphosed since he had passed on the way to the engine room. It was no longer polished carved wood. The gray steel fire door had been swung into place and welded closed.

Katz could barely hear the voices on the other side as the computer geniuses gave way to panic. They tried to attract attention by rapping on the door and shouting.

"Attention all passengers," the intercom blared. "Move directly to your lifeboat stations. We are abandoning ship. I repeat, we are abandoning ship immediately."

Katz suddenly understood. He knew the entire plot. From the beginning Vulcan had been intent on murdering five hundred of the western world's top computer experts. Their deaths would set back the U.S. and its allies for decades, and the KGB would never be suspected. His defeat in his Cheyenne was trivial compared to the coup he was in the process of pulling.

Vulcan's evil brilliance was mind-boggling. When Phoenix Force had gotten in the way, Vulcan had set them up to take the blame. They would probably be touted after the tragic event as fanatic terrorists.

The intercom blared again. "This is your captain speaking. Abandon ship." The voice lacked professional control. No doubt Vulcan had taken the bridge and was creating chaos. Fear and a few gunmen would turn aside any heroic attempts to save the men and women in the auditorium. Vulcan's plan was working.

"Oh, God," Katz groaned as the water reached his knees. The water was probably as deep on the other side.

Before he could think, the other four teammates crowded in beside him. The three biggest men were bleeding from injuries they had received when they squeezed themselves through the ragged sides of the engine room door. They all wanted out. They could see the stairs leading to survival.

"Katz," McCarter said, breathing heavily from exertion. "What are you doing here? Let's get out of this bathtub. I don't have a rubber ducky. Come on."

"Can't." Katz motioned toward the auditorium. "They're welded in."

"Oh, no," McCarter said. "The poor bastards are all going to drown."

"Not if I can help it."

"What the hell can we do?" Manning asked. "Neither percussion nor fragment grenades would dent that steel."

"Go find another welding setup, McCarter."

"What?"

"You heard me. Talk to the crew. Anybody who might know how to open this door."

"That's crazy. What chance have I got to find—"

"Not much, but we have got to try," Katz remarked as he looked McCarter in the eye.

The Englishman subsided. "Okay, I'll look for something, but don't keep these other guys down here to drown for a hopeless cause."

Katz slapped him on the shoulder and warned him as he left, "Keep your gun handy. I just killed one of Vulcan's men."

"So I can see." McCarter stepped over the body and was gone.

"Stand back," Katz told the others.

They moved around the corner, and Katz fired three times at the weld. Although he had ducked aside, the bullets bounced harmlessly off the metal, and he nearly killed himself with a ricocheting bullet.

The water reached his thighs, and the cries from inside grew louder.

"It's no good," Encizo said. "I'll stay down here and drown with you if you want, Katz, but we have to have a torch. And McCarter hasn't a chance of finding one without knowing where to look."

"You know who's in there? You know what this means?"

"Yeah," James said. "It means Russia could get a reliable defense against nuclear weapons before we do. Eventually they could incinerate any country without fear of retaliation."

Katz shouted again. "Their deaths mean the space program is dead. It means thousands, maybe millions will die because the free world no longer has the brains to design new medical technology."

"Okay," Manning said. "I'll search the goddamned ship until I have to swim from one place to another. But we are not going to find an acetylene setup in time."

"I'll go with you," James agreed.

The two had reached the companionway leading up when Katz smiled. When he had understood Vulcan's plan, it was as though he had gained a way of knowing how the man's mind worked, as if he could read it.

He could figure out exactly where the evil genius would hide the evidence.

"I know where the welding gear is."

Both men looked at him doubtfully. "Where?" Manning asked.

"In my suite or one of yours."

"Huh?"

"You heard me. My suite. And Encizo, look up some diving gear."

"Like what?"

"Air tanks, breathing apparatus. We may be working underwater before this is over."

Alone, Yakov Katzenelenbogen sat down on the step halfway up.

He was tired and had to get his second wind while he had a chance. He felt sure Manning and James would be back in time to free the computer scientists. The water rose more slowly since it had more space to engulf.

Above him he could hear the panic lessening. Most people were outside, he guessed, in the lifeboats, on the deck, or leaping over the side with or without life jackets. There was no immediate necessity to abandon ship, but he felt positive that Vulcan had brought as many people as he had in order to instigate the panic needed for cover.

Reaching for a cigarette, he found his packet soaked, and it fell apart in his hands.

Maybe Vulcan's soldier had a pack. Katz checked the body of the man he had shot. He found a dry pack of Viceroy's and a book of matches.

He sat down again and held the barrel of his gun under his left arm and lit up.

He started to turn when he heard footsteps, but he saw the gun too late to duck for cover.

Arnold Vulcan and Ann Cardwell were on the steps behind him. Katz did not look at them once he knew their position. And he could see them in a four-inch square of a brass wall decoration ahead of him.

"So you escaped," Vulcan said. "I am sorry your freedom will be so short-lived."

"Wait," Katz pleaded. "Let a man finish his last cigarette, at least." He exhaled and held the cigarette with his lips. He had also made an almost imperceptible move across his body with his artificial hand without the movement being noticed.

"How much will you bet that you've overlooked one little thing, Reverend Vulcan?" he shot the question at the KGB man.

"No stalling. Take your last puff."

"What did he overlook?" Ann Cardwell asked.

Katz let the cigarette drop from his lips.

"The gun muzzle barely poking out of my armpit," Katz said dryly as he pulled the trigger.

The powder flame burned his skin.

The gun recoiled, and he barely managed to keep his grip.

The slug drilled into Vulcan's stomach. He fired reflexively, the bullet burying itself into the acoustic tile in the ceiling. He dropped the weapon, needing both hands to catch the blood and innards pouring from his middle. His only expression was surprise.

He rolled down the steps and bumped against his killer.

Katz stepped aside and had already covered the Cardwell woman. She called out to him, "No. Don't shoot."

She dropped a gun she had taken from her purse.

"I want to defect!" she cried.

"Kick both guns down here and sit down," Katz ordered her.

"But the water is rising."

"Sit. You get out of this alive only if we save every one of the computer people."

Then all of the team except Encizo were back, Manning and James bringing the big torch, masks, and the large double cylinders.

McCarter was back, too, carrying a household-size welder kit. "Well," he grumbled. "It's all I could find."

Manning, standing in water up to his middle, released acetylene from one cylinder, then let the oxygen flow out to make the mixture he needed. With a flint he turned the combined flow into a spear of flame.

He waded into the water and started cutting as high as he could reach. The water kept rising. When he had a slot cut across the top, he was standing on his tiptoes.

He started on one of the two vertical cuts he needed.

McCarter insisted on using his small torch to cut fractions of an inch per minute from the left-hand side of the door.

Knowing his torch flame would continue cutting underwater, Manning held his breath and ducked beneath the surface. He could cut an inch or less before he had to pop up again. Calvin James moved in beside him and they tried taking turns, but they were losing the battle.

In desperation James surfaced and spoke to Katz who was now in the water, too, while watching Ann Cardwell who showed no interest in escaping.

"Face it," Calvin said. "We might manage to make a smaller hole than we want. We'd save everybody but a few fatties. And we'd save ourselves, too."

From inside came the anguished cries of the trapped people.

"Oh, hell," James said as he went back underwater. He could not bring himself to quit, but when he came up again he yelled. "Where's that scuba gear?"

"Somebody call my name?" Encizo cried out, running up and carrying two Aqua-lung kits. "Courtesy of the sport shop, guys."

"Toss them," Katz yelled. "Seconds count."

A moment later James and Manning donned the equipment and ducked below the surface. They didn't surface again until Katz could hear the bending of metal and the screams of hope. The entire team were in for the final push.

They broke through together.

Moments later a motley contingent of computer experts—conservative business types, others who looked like part of the rock music scene—took turns to climb through the hole in the steel door and run up the companionway.

They distributed thanks to everybody they saw, including Ann Cardwell.

They were still exiting the auditorium when Katz called his men together. "Time to get off this thing," he said, "before we end up getting asked a million questions."

The other team members followed, with Ann Cardwell tagging after them.

Katz tried not to look at the disaster panic had caused. Inevitably there were casualties. Some lived, immobilized by broken bones. A few heroes remained behind.

Katz quickly gave quiet but firm directions to some people who could organize what still remained of the evacuation, then made that hard decision. He could stay to the last minute, heroically save someone, and get his picture on TV.

But now he could rely on others to do that because publicity could be as lethal as bullets to Phoenix Force.

Ironically, although there were people floating about in their life jackets, many lifeboats remained on their racks.

"We'll take that one," Katz said. He pointed to a partially covered craft with an inboard engine. Climbing aboard, he checked it out. There were provisions for days, maybe weeks, and it was supplied with navigational equipment.

They would find an island and land during the day. They had the skill and experience to blend with the other tourists and make their way back to the States with Hal Brognola's help.

With the hull in the water, the teammates slid down the rope.

In the confusion all around them, Calvin James had to get Katz's attention. Ann Cardwell was still on the slanting deck.

"You're not leaving me. I told you I'd defect. I can name a hundred agents. Please."

He unlatched the last cable and motioned for James to start the motor.

"This boat's filled," he yelled to her. "Sorry, lady."

Only Calvin James was surprised.

"You're not leaving her?" he said. "She wants to defect. You can't let her die."

"She'll survive. She'll find a hero," Katz said. "Her kind always does. And she'll defect. What else can she do?"

"But—"

"Take a course of one, eight, zero," David McCarter said. "Go north or south in these waters, and you'll hit land soon enough."

For minutes the men rode silently until they were well clear of the people and debris in the water.

They saw two freighters already heading toward the *Odyssey*.

"We ought to stay out of sight for a while," Encizo said. "Some remote island. After all, I think we really earned a cushy vacation, haven't we?"